Your]

-A Novel Written by-
KC Blaze

Copyright © 2014 by True Glory Publications
Published by True Glory Publications LLC
Join Our Mailing List by texting TrueGlory at 95577

www.urbanfictionnews.com

platinumfiction@yahoo.com

Twitter: @26kessa

This novel is a work of fiction. Any resemblances to actual events, real people, living or dead, organizations, establishments or locales are products of the author's imagination. Other names, characters, places, and incidents are used fictitiously.

Cover Design: Michael Horne
Editor: Kylar Bradshaw

All rights reserved. No part of this book may be used or reproduced in any form or by any means electronic or mechanical, including photocopying, recording or by information storage and retrieval system, without the written permission from the publisher and writer.

Because of the dynamic nature of the Internet, any Web addresses or links contained in this book may have changed since publication, and may no longer be valid. The views expressed in this work are solely those of the author and do not necessarily reflect the views of the publisher and the publisher hereby disclaims any responsibility for them.

Table of Contents

Say What Now?...............1
More Hurt than Happy...........7
Master Mind Control..........16
House Hunting..............24
Time for the Talk............40
Unbelievable Stupidity...........50
Father Figure..............57
Tough Love...............70
Playing Catch Up............83
Unresolved Isuues............91
Déjà vu................103
Moving Day..............110
Almost Back to Nromal..........119
Working on Me.............129
Little Bundles of Possibilities.......143
The Green Eyed Monster.........156
Divorce Meetings............164
A Small World After All.........168
Dr. Appointments............173
House Warming Gifts..........179
Murder on My Mind...........190
The Unthinkable............197
Finding Answers............206
Hope in the Midst of Tragedy.......212
See No Evil..............230
Rude Awakening............232
As it Relates to Guilt..........247
Mind over Matter............254
Daddy's Girl..............256
Harmless?...............261

Blame it on my Hormones.........................265
Please Don't..278
And His Name is Justin..........................280
If Ever a Time......................................290
Caught Slipping...................................292
The Good News....................................296
Settling Matters...................................301
Paternity Matters.................................306
Lingering Guilt....................................312
Testing, Testing and then Results..............319
Speechless..323

Your Husband, My Man 3

Written by:
K.C Blaze

Acknowledgments

People always thank God as an afterthought to their success. I want to acknowledge God and what he's done for me by saying thank you for giving me wisdom, thank you for allowing me to test my faith. Thank you for saying yes when others have said no. I would like to also thank my family, it's not easy dealing with me and my drive. I appreciate you allowing me to be me. A special thanks to Jae. Easley who helped me with the inevitable writers block. Your feedback and willingness to talk things out with me is greatly appreciated and not taken for granted. I want to thank everyone who's ever picked up a copy of my books, left a review or supported my work. Every author's dream is to have someone read their work and care enough to comment. So thank you all! A special thank you goes to Shameek Speight. I want to thank you for seeing my potential and telling me so. I respect your vision and appreciate your grind!

Say What Now?
Misha

What felt like an explosion just went off in my head causing my ears to ring loudly, I couldn't believe the words that just left my soon to be ex-husband's mouth. If my ears didn't fail me, Tori just said he was taking the Adoption center to court for our son. I quickly stood up from the table leaving a stunned Arnold Blake in my wake.

"Tori? What are you thinking?" I spoke at his back. He spun around to face me.

"Look Misha, I get it ok? I fucked up, but our son, *my* son, doesn't have to pay for our mistakes." His words were no longer filled with venom, but a calm that scared me.

"Tori, he isn't paying for anything. He has a loving family that has been raising him all of his life." I tried to reason with him.

"Do you understand that I'm not asking for your permission? I am going to get my son back whether it's with you or not." He turned and walked towards the exit. I didn't follow him I just walked back into the office to see what I could do.

"Arnold?" was the only word that left my mouth.

"You never mentioned a kid Misha." Arnold looked insulted like I offended him personally.

After his assistant left the room, I told Arnold about the adoption back when I was eighteen and he let me know that Tori may have a case if he never signed away his parental rights or consent to the adoption. I couldn't believe this was coming back to haunt me. I didn't want to overwhelm our son and I definitely didn't want to rip him from the only family he's ever known. I would need to do something and quick before Tori went through with this. The one thing I knew about my husband was that he could be persistent as hell when he wanted something.

"So what do we do now?" I sat in my chair placing my face in my hands while asking questions I really wasn't sure I wanted an answer to.

"Well right now if you want to continue pursuing the divorce in spite of what he's said, then we can proceed." Arnold shuffled paperwork looking more lost than I've ever seen him.

"I need to think this through." I confessed I couldn't make decisions with this hanging over my head. "I need time to think about all of this, but I'll contact you when I've come to a decision." I said as I stood up to leave. I was so sure of everything a few minutes ago and now I feel like I am losing my mind. One thing was for sure, I need to contact Julie from the adoption center ASAP. I couldn't leave Arnold's office fast enough.

In order to allow the adoption to go through, I had to tell the agency that the child's father was unknown. This could get real sticky, real quick. I wasn't going to tell my mother about this meeting cause it would provoke an all-night prayer meeting. I stepped into the rented Altima and looked around before pulling off in the direction of the nearest convenience store to get a newspaper. This can't slow down my plans of moving out. With the creator of the she-devil staying at my mother's house, I knew I wouldn't be able to stay there for too much longer.

I pulled into a gas station and grabbed my purse before going in to buy a paper. The jingle of the bells hanging above the door announced my entrance. I scanned the store with my eyes quickly and walked over to the dwindling stack of today's papers.

"Misha?" a familiar voice asked. I turned around to see my brother's friend, Eric.

"Oh hey Eric, how are you?" I asked non-chalantly. Eric has been trying to talk to me since I was a teenager, but my brother would much rather kill him then see him succeed at that.

"You looking good. Where you on your way to?" he asked like he had the right.

"Why you need to know?" I asked a bit sarcastically with just enough seductiveness to not make him offended.

"Oh, excuse me gorgeous. I was just trying to start a conversation. Here, what you getting?" He reached out his hand and placed a dollar on the counter to pay for my paper.

"Thanks"

"No problem, if you stop playing, I'd be more than willing to pay for dinner." Eric responded.

"Sure, set the date with my brother." I walked away smiling.

"Awww, you know you're not right." He laughed with his eyes glued to my ass. I sat in my car searching through the paper for the classified ads. My eyes finally reached the rental properties section pretty quick. Stopping immediately at a two bedroom, two bathroom apartment complete with a community swimming pool in the downtown section of Atlanta. I circled the listing and reached for my cell to schedule a viewing. As I started to dial, the nagging sensation to call Tori bombarded my thoughts.

More Hurt than Happy
Tori

I thought I would feel on top of the world after telling Misha what I was planning on doing; but after saying it, I felt more like an ass than a victor. After walking away, I sat in my car for a few minutes half wishing Misha would follow me, but she didn't. So I pulled off in the direction of home. I was going to call my family lawyer and discuss my options. I meant what I said about getting my son if that wasn't an option, I at least wanted to be able to see him, to touch him.

Driving through my block and pulling into the driveway, left me feeling more alone than I've ever felt. This felt different from knowing Misha was at her mom's or out with friends this felt permanent. Even when we were separated and I was considering me and Lauren I didn't feel this alone coming home. I guess I always felt like I would have Misha around and Lauren was deeply involved in my life, so I never had time to feel lonely. My cell started ringing and I saw my favorite picture of Misha flash across the screen. I couldn't stop myself from smiling.

"Hello." I tried not to sound too happy.

"Tori we need to talk." She stated.

"Well, I'm home so you can come here." I offered.

"No, I think we should meet somewhere public." I wanted to laugh out loud but contained myself.

"I'm not coming back out." I played hardball.

"Fine, I'll be there in thirty minutes. Please have the door unlocked." She gave me orders which surprisingly felt good.

"Fine." I heard a beep that indicated she ended the call.

I grabbed my car keys and headed out to get her favorite peach iced tea. I didn't give a damn how this was going to work, but I was going to have my wife.

I was back home within ten minutes. A plan started formulating in my mind and I decided to give it a try. I waited til about ten minutes before she was to get here and unlocked the front door and went into the kitchen to start making dinner. I would start cooking and invite her to eat while she was already here. She loved my Salmon pinwheels. I heard the door open and close a few minutes later.

"Tori?" Misha called out.

"I'm in the kitchen." I answered.

"Did I interrupt you?" she asked while setting her purse down on the kitchen table and taking a seat.

"No, I was hungry so I decided to cook."

"What are you making? You know what never mind it doesn't matter."

"Salmon pinwheels to answer your question." I turned to see her expression. She gave me a knowing glance before sucking her teeth. I washed my hands and walked over to where she sat.

"No worries, I have enough for two." I said before bending low to remove her heels.

"I'm not staying that long." She answered with no resistance.

"I know, but we can still eat right?" I asked hoping my plan to seduce her ass to stay was working.

"Tori, what happened back there?" Just like Misha she cut to the chase.

"Can we talk about that while we eat? I don't want to burn my food." I dodged the question.

"Fine." I could feel her eyes burning through my back.

"You thirsty? I got your favorite peach tea." I asked without looking her way.

"Yes please."

I reached for a glass and poured her a cup of iced tea and sat it in front of her.

"Do you remember the first time I made you my world famous salmon pinwheels?" I asked.

"Yes, I remember you bragging and showing off about your cooking skills." She laughed before drinking from her cup.

"Bragging? Showing off? I have major skills in the kitchen. Had you begging me to make them every night." Her laugh filled the kitchen and broke my heart before putting it back together again.

"I wasn't begging you, you wished I begged. You are such a drama king." She continued her playful rant.

"Please big daddy make those salmon cakes again." I joked making her laugh uncontrollably.

"You are such a lie."

"I'm lying? Tell me that to my face." I walked over to within an inch of her face making her breath catch in her throat.

"Go head tell me to my face." Any closer and my lips would have touched hers.

"I didn't call you that and I never begged." I moved my lips closer so hers. Her lips were brushing against mine with each word she spoke. By the end of her sentence, I was kissing her soft lips. Her eyes closed slowly. I used my tongue to part her lips and traced the lining of her mouth. She tasted as good as I remembered.

"Tori, the food." She gently pushed me away and pointed toward the stove.

"You're lucky I don't want to ruin my culinary reputation." I backed away.

"Oh whatever." She continued to drink her tea.

"I'm moving out of my mom's house soon. I started apartment hunting." Misha changed the subject. I didn't know if she was trying to test me, but her words cut deep.

"Oh yeah?" I played it off.

"I think I may have found something." She continued.

"You can always come back home." I turned to face her, but she looked down.

"But we're in the middle of a divorce." She finally answered.

"Look I'm gonna keep this real with you. I don't want to end our marriage. I want to work it out with you. I realize my mistake and losing you would fuck me up in the head. If you feel like you want time away from me, I understand; but getting an apartment and signing a lease is too much for me to handle, Misha seriously. But I'm not the only one who fucked up here we both did. You really don't want me no more?" I was being real serious and didn't break eye contact.

"To be honest Tori, I do want you and our marriage and spending time with you like this makes things more confusing, but I'm not ready to act like everything is normal when the reality is it's not." Just as honest as I dished it, she served it back at me.

"Fair enough, can we just agree to not make any serious decisions until we're both sure it's really over?" I asked not really contemplating the end of my marriage.

I finished dinner and set it on the table. It smelled like a million dollars. Misha found a thousand reasons to bring me back to the divorce meeting. I wasn't going to give up my entire hand though. Not until I was sure we were working things out.

"I meant what I said about getting our son. Right now, I'm not sure if I want to sue for custody or if I just want to ask for visitation. I can't live in a world where we aren't complete. I vowed to never let my children think I didn't want them and because I didn't really have a say in it I'm going to fight for what's mine." I finished talking, but I noticed Misha stopped eating somewhere in the middle of it.

"He has a family that has been raising him from birth and if we mess with that it could devastate him. He has friends and a life where he is Tori." She reasoned and her point was valid, but I needed to look him in the eye and see that he was alright.

Master Mind Control
Lauren

Sitting in my living room, I tried to make sense of my life up til this point. It was hard to believe that just a few short months ago I was living an oblivious life of blissful ignorance. For the first time in a long time I set on my couch in silence. No television, no music just me and my thoughts. After talking things over with Chris about handling my dad, I decided that I needed to think things over before speaking with my father again. There is still a lot going on there that I need to figure out. I don't know what happened to Shannon and not too sure I give a damn. Being alone never felt this horrible.

The buzz of my intercom let me know I had a visitor. My heart sped up, I couldn't take any more surprises. I eased off the couch and over to the small white box beside the front door.

"Who is it?" I asked.

"Lauren it's me." My father's voice spoke through the intercom. I didn't want to talk to him. He was a rapist and attempted murderer of the one woman I've been dying to get to know.

"Go away Dad." I answered.

"Lauren, I need you to let me explain. You think you know it all, but you don't." He tried to reason with me.

"What did you do to Shannon?" I asked forgetting that I wasn't supposed to know that she was there.

"Shannon is fine. Open the gate honey." I heard the pleading in his voice and tears began to stream down my face as I hit the open button to the gate. I wanted normalcy, I wanted my father back the man who raised me. I needed him back. I heard his car's tires against the cement before he parked. Moments later a light knock on the door indicated he was outside. I hesitated to open it.

My father stood on the other side of the door. His arm in a sling, his eyes staring down at the floor. I've never seen him look so pathetic. I stepped aside for him to enter. He followed behind me to the couch.

"Lauren listen." His voice came just above a whisper. For the first time I realized that my father lost his power, what made him great was his cloak of mystery that once surrounded him. He was no longer the man he painted himself to be, but now stood the common, ordinary Loren Michaels brother of the Great Joseph Michaels. I couldn't bring myself to look at him no matter how hard I tried. "I know things look bad right now, but it's important that you tell me where your mother is." He continued.

I couldn't believe he was still trying to find her after all that happened.

"Dad, I need you to stop ok? You're trying to find my mom when Shannon tried to burn down my club with me in it." His head jerked back like I just punched him in his face.

"What?" he asked.

"It was Shannon who tried to burn down my club and set my Jaguar on fire. So while you think my mother is the enemy, it was really your trifling ass fiancé." I shouted unintentionally. He started to pace my living room floor like he was going to lose his mind.

"How do you know it was Shannon?" he asked through clenched teeth.

"Because I overheard her talking to Arnold in his office. She said she couldn't believe he was sleeping with a selfish brat like me and that it was bad enough she had to share him with her sister and that the next time she would do more than burn down my club." I didn't feel right telling him everything, but I needed to get his mind off my mom.

Without another word, he walked out of my condo and back into his car. I ran behind him.

"Dad, where are you going?" I asked, but he didn't answer just continued to his car like he didn't hear me.

"Dad? What are you about to do?" I continued my questions. He finally shouted over his shoulder.

"Nothing, I'll contact you later. It's not over with your mom. I'll explain later. Lauren trust me." With that, he closed his car door and sped in reverse before charging forward to the gate. I ran back to the house and hit the gate's open button. I didn't want him damaging it on his way out.

Life was getting overwhelming and I hated not having anyone to talk to about it when I remembered Tori. I was shocked when Chris said he stopped by and I wondered what he could have wanted. I shook the desire to call or text him. I didn't want to ruin my mom's chances of being safe. Even though I secretly hoped he wanted to tell me that he realized Misha wasn't the one for him.

A strong feeling that my father was potentially dangerous made me quiver involuntarily. With my club still being repaired, I had no asylum, no place to drown out my loneliness. I picked up the remote and turned the television on, flipping the channels until I came across my club's commercial. In the same moment I wanted to change the channel I thought about Charles Johnson, Arnold's investor friend. I jumped up from the couch and started looking around for a copy of the agreement we all made for them to invest. Twenty minutes later I located and spotted the card with Charles' name and numbers. I grabbed my cell and twirled the card between my fingers debating on if I should call or not.

    I decided to dial the number that read cell and hit the green phone button before I could change my mind.

    "Hello?" A deep and sexy voice answered moments later.

    "Uh, hello may I speak with Charles please?" I asked a bit hesitant not really sure I knew what I would say was the reason for this call.

    "This is he, whose calling please?" he asked.

"Hi, its Lauren Michael's from Club Seduction."

"Yes, how are you? Can you give me a moment?" His voice lowered faintly which was a clear indicator he didn't want someone to hear his conversation.

"Sure." I listened carefully to the sounds of a door closing in his background and his footsteps hitting against the floor.

"I'm back, how are you though, Lauren?" he asked again.

"I'm ok, all things considered. Were you busy? Have I interrupted you?" I asked more to gather information than to actually know.

"No, no I'm fine just wasn't expecting your call is all. Is everything ok?" he seemed a bit concerned, but his voice was still engaging enough to want to talk.

"Everything is fine. I wanted to know if your offer of a drink still stands." I flirted more directly.

I could tell he was smiling which made me smile.

"That offer always stands."

"Good, would tonight be a bad time to take you up on it?" I loved the cat and mouse game and felt my seductive juices begin to rise again.

"Tonight would be perfect. I can pick you up in an hour." Charles offered.

"Perfect. Can we meet in front of Seduction?" she asked.

"Sure, see you then beautiful." He complimented before hanging up. I need a distraction and there is something about Charles that says he is up for the job.

House Hunting
Misha

Tori made his position known and for the first time since our lives crumbled I feel like I'm on the same page. I decided to look for apartments that allowed me a month to month lease. This would give me the flexibility of leaving if we decided to work things out. After eating dinner, reminiscing and fighting our still strong physical attraction toward one another, I left to go back to my mother's house. I dreaded going into the house knowing the woman that helped create Lauren was still there. When I pulled up, my brother Jerry was outside. He walked up to my car before I could get out.

"Misha, what the fuck is going on? Why is mom letting her stay here?" His expression was serious mixed with a little confusion.

"I really don't know, but I'm moving out Jerry. I'm not staying here with trifling ass Lauren's mom here." I answered.

"I heard them talking today and Lauren's mom was saying that her dad really is trying to kill her."

"What? Did you hear what for?" I asked momentarily stunned. Her whole family is messed up, which explains a whole lot.

"Nah, I was irked that I couldn't walk around in my boxers, so I stepped outside. She seems nice though." He looked down when he said that. I guess he knew he was committing a form of betrayal by not saying she was a she devil like her daughter. I pushed my car door open and stepped out.

"Well, nice or not, I can't stand her." I said while slamming the car door shut.

"I'm going over to my girl's house. I need to get outta here." Jerry walked toward his car leaving me with nothing but my thoughts. I did a slow walk over to the front door and entered with caution. I could hear my mother talking in the kitchen, but I went upstairs to my room. I slipped into my pajamas without showering. I didn't want to admit to myself that I loved Tori's scent on my body. I laid beneath the covers thinking about our conversation, but it was hard to fight the feeling of being excited about getting my own place. I went from my mother's house to living with Tori and I wanted to know what living on my own actually felt like. Moments later I was drifting to sleep with thoughts of freedom and the possibility of dating my husband again.

    A soft knocking on the door made me shift in my sleep.

    "Misha, are you up?" Diane's head peeked through the door. I sat up quickly, a bit irritated that she would come in before allowing me to welcome her in.

    "I am now." I answered sarcastically.

"I just wanted to come in to talk to you for a little bit. Your mother told me a bit of what happened." She walked in and actually walked toward my bed and took a seat. I wanted to shove her off onto the floor.

"There really is nothing to talk about. Lauren is the most self-centered woman I know and she has everything handed to her because she tosses her pussy around so I shouldn't be so surprised that she wanted to have my husband too." I vented.

"Misha I'm sorry about what she's done to you. I know that it must be painful."

"Painful Ha! Painful is an understatement. Your daughter stole my life from me." I shouted at the Lauren look alike.

My mother popped her head into the room. "Is everything ok in here?" she asked, concern written across her aging face.

"Yeah, I was just leaving." Diane stood up to leave and I jumped out of bed. I needed to get out of this house. My mother read the look on my face.

"Misha, what's the problem honey?" she closed the door behind her.

"Mom, I can't be here not with her here. I have to go, I'm looking for an apartment." I spoke while sliding on a pair of jeans and a pink tank top shirt.

"Where are my shoes?" I asked no one in particular.

"You don't think you're moving too fast?" My mother asked.

"Mama, I know you want me to be here forever, but I really need to be on my own." I kissed her on her cheek and started walking toward the bedroom door.

"Well, I need you back here today around seven if you don't mind. I have a surprise for you all." My mother yelled at my back. I nodded my agreement and jogged down the stairs and out the door.

I headed in the direction of the Viera Briarcliff apartment complex. I was meeting with a woman by the name of Susan Leslie. I was bright eyed driving through the neighborhood with tall trees, well-manicured lawns and gorgeously designed homes. I parked in the apartment complex parking lot and waited for Susan to show up. Being early meant I had a little time on my hands to get a feel for the neighborhood. My cell pinged indicating a text message. It was Tori saying good morning. I smiled and sent good morning in return. It felt weird house hunting without him. A red Ford Focus pulled into the parking lot beside me with blonde haired woman wearing large sunglasses. Something told me it was Susan. I stepped out of my car to find out.

"Susan?" I asked. The woman turned in my direction.

"Yes, are you Misha?" she asked extending her hand.

"Yes I am. I'm sorry for being early." I apologized while shaking her hand.

"No, no don't worry about it. I'm actually glad that you've come early. The apartment is ready for us to do the walk through." She hit the alarm on her keys to lock her car door and I followed her up into the leasing office to get the apartments keys.

"So, were you looking for one or two bedrooms?" Susan asked over her shoulder.

"I'm interested in two bedrooms. I have lots of clothes." I joked and we both shared a knowing smile. She grabbed the keys from behind the desk.

"Ok so follow me." We walked through a set of glass doors and I couldn't help but look around. There were two peach colored chairs in front of a marble fireplace. A large tree with banana leaves sat in an oversized planter beside the fireplace.

"Right here is the community center. Residents are free to sit in here and chat. Next door is the gym, we just got a whole line of new equipment. You would have access to the gym from five in the morning until ten p.m. Monday thru Friday and eight a.m. to seven p.m. on the weekend. We do have a pool." Susan continued to show me around. I felt like a kid in the candy store finally able to touch the goodies behind the counter.

Finally, she led me to an elevator where she continued to talk until we reached the second floor. When the doors opened, she continued her talk only this time talking about the quirks of some of the neighbors.

"Here you go." She pointed toward room 210. I loved the color scheme in each of the rooms. A large floor plan meant I would have lots of room for my clothes.

"So Mrs. Carter how soon were you looking to move in?" Susan asked.

"I was hoping to move in right away."

"Are you currently employed?" she asked politely.

"Yes, I'm a secretary at an attorney's office."

"How long have you been employed with them?" She continued her questioning.

"Well, I've just started, but I have a letter showing my salary." I reached inside of my handbag for the letter.

"We will have to run your credit also."

Her words were beginning to feel more like a pile of bricks falling on my chest. Most of my credit is tied up with Tori. I don't have individual credit.

"It shouldn't be a problem however, I'm in the process of getting a divorce, so I'm not altogether sure of how that will look. I do have the down payment, first, last, and security as well." I tried to help my odds.

"There is a possibility that we may need a co-signer." Susan informed me, making my heart drop where I stood. I needed to get out of my mother's house. I told her I'd still like to go through the application process and decided to cross my fingers. The apartment was perfect something I could see Lauren living in. That thought made me feel good that I could actually have something she could have.

Susan and I went back to the front office where I filled out the application and gave her a check that would cover holding the apartment while we went through the credit check process. She told me she would get back to me in two days after giving me a receipt for the deposit. I walked back to the car feeling a bit sad. I really wanted to get my own spot. A quick look at my cell let me know that I had another message. Tori asked if I wanted to meet with him for lunch. I told him yes right before sending Vivian a message. I needed to talk with someone about my possible dilemma. She responded by saying I could stop by her house around four thirty. I sent ok before driving toward Tori's job. I debated on telling him about needing a co-signer because I knew he would say I should just come home instead.

Traffic was still light from people being at work and children being in school. I tried to find a parking spot near his work, but as usual there was nothing and the parking lot was reserved for employees and clients only. I slipped into a spot a few blocks down and sent him an I'm here text. If Tori and I work out he would have to prove to me that he really wanted me back. Cheating wasn't just a blow to man's ego. Minutes later he sent a where are you message and I drove up to the door to his building. There he stood smoking hot in a gray suit with the purple tie I got him for his birthday. I hit the unlock button as he reached for the passenger door.

"I feel overdressed." He leaned in to kiss me which was common, but I gave him my cheek instead. Without hesitation, he pressed his lips into my skin.

His cologne filled my rental making me inhale deeply.

"I can go change if you have time." I offered.

"Are you kidding me, you'll get me fired. You know how long it takes you to get ready." He joked.

"Whatever, then where would you like to go?" I asked.

"Anywhere you'd like to go." His eyes bore into my skin.

"Well let's see, you're dressed too nice for bar-b-que and I'm underdressed for anything fancy, so let's go to The Varsity." I suggested one of our favorite hot dog spots. Though the lines are insanely long they move quickly.

"That's fine by me." Tori agreed and so I headed in the direction of The Varsity. I wanted to flip the radio on, but he turned it off and reached over to touch my hair.

"What are you doing?" I asked.

"Nothing, just looking at you. I can't look at you now?" he asked playfully.

"You're not just looking though you're touching." I kept my eyes on the road.

"What? I can't touch you either?" he asked with his fingers still in my hair. I didn't protest, he would do it anyway, so I tried to relax and shake the feeling of irritation from this morning.

Just like I thought the line at The Varsity was long, but good thing they had curbside service. We were able to place an order ten minutes after pulling up. It took fifteen minutes for it to get to us. We ate in the car and people-watched like we used to in high school.

"I miss you." He stated between bites of his food. I stopped eating to look at him.

"What?" I asked.

"I really miss you. Your big mouth, your crazy ass jokes, even your messed up attitude." He continued.

"Good." I answered. I tried to act like I didn't give a damn, but it felt good knowing that he still cared about me. I missed him too, but I wasn't ready for him to know that.

"How was your day?" he asked.

"A bit disappointing but ok I guess."

"Why disappointing?" He finished his hotdog and started wiping his suit from possible crumbs.

"Well first Lauren's mom woke me up trying to make me feel bad then." I started but he cut me off.

"Lauren's mom?" he looked surprised.

"You heard me right. Her mom is staying at my mom's house because her dad is trying to kill her." I forgot he didn't know about Lauren stopping by mom's house the other day.

"What the fuck? Are you serious?" His voice elevated.

"Yes, that's why I gotta go like asap." I answered. I tried to read his face but he looked angry. There was no telling what exactly he was angry about.

"Damn, her ass is bold as shit." He spoke aloud more to himself than to me. I started the car and headed back toward his office.

"Look, I'm sorry Mish, you can come back home." He pressed.

"Tori, we already had this discussion and I'm not ready ok so drop it for now please." I didn't feel like having the same conversation again. When I pulled up to his office building, I noticed a clear parking spot in front. I pulled in slowly.

"When can I see you again?" Tori asked.

"I'm not sure." I needed to play hard to get to give myself some time to think this apartment situation through.

"Ok, how about tonight?" he continued pressing.

"Tori." He moved forward and kissed me, stopping my thoughts before they came out of my mouth.

"You know you want to." He spoke between kisses. He was right about that, physically I was highly attracted to him and my lower region began to scream for me to agree, but it wasn't about her right now.

"I'll think about it." I answered.

"Ok tonight around seven. I'll see you there." He opened the door quickly, getting out of the car before I could disagree.

"I didn't say." I screamed to his back as he jogged away from the car.

"I can't hear you." He yelled over his shoulder.

I pulled off and drove toward another apartment I circled in yesterday's paper. My enthusiasm completely depleted.

Time for the Talk
Tori

Hearing Misha say Lauren's mom was at her mom's crib made me want to snap. Lauren's persistent ass was making things more difficult. It felt good spending time with my wife like old times even though she was acting a bit distant. If I knew Misha, I knew nothing would be easy, but I was willing to fight through it if it meant I had her in the end. When I got back to my office, I closed the door behind me, just for it to be opened again by Kimberly the office flirt. She had a few papers in her hand.

"Yes?" I asked politely.

"Did you already get the company memo?" she asked with a smile on her face.

"Uh." I looked around my desk to see if I had it. The company insisted on handing out paper memo's stating most of us didn't read non-project related emails.

"I don't think so." I looked up when I couldn't find it. She walked over to my desk a little bit more sway in her hips than usual.

"Well here you go then." Her cleavage was very noticeable as she leaned across the desk to hand me my memo. I thanked her, trying to keep my eyes diverted though it was a bit challenging. It was no secret that Kimberly was attractive, but it was also well known that she was scoping candidates with potential advancement opportunities as well. She had the attention of many of the eligible and not so eligible brothas in the office.

As soon as she left, I reached for my cell phone and sent Lauren a message. 'We need to talk' the message read. I need to put Lauren in her place despite my previous moment of weakness. It wasn't until it was time for me to leave that she responded with an 'I know.' I knew I couldn't invite her to my house so I asked her to meet me at the only spot I knew we would not be seen. Our old quickie spot behind the bushes near the park by my house. She agreed and when the clock struck four I headed to the parking garage for my Challenger. I needed to ask what Lauren was thinking about when she went to Misha's mom for help. I also needed to tell her to back off because her involvement is making my wife hesitant about coming back to me.

I felt confident that if I was able to reason with her that we could resolve things in an adult manner. I made it to our old spot around four thirty. Her BMW wasn't anywhere to be found. I debated on taking off my suit jacket or leaving it on. I decided to take it off and laid it across the backseat. A light tap on my car window let me know she had arrived. I hit the unlock button and she opened and sat inside wearing a thin black rain jacket cinched at the waist.

"Hey." She spoke first.

"Hey, what's going on" My question was more from nerves than actually giving a damn.

"Chris told me you stopped by the other day." She stared at me.

"Uh yeah, I can't remember why now. I brought you here because I really think we need to talk." She reached her hand over and rested it in my lap.

"I know." She said.

"No you don't know. I think it's fucked up that you asked your mom to stay at Misha's." I went in trying not to lose sight of my original intention.

"What? You don't know what you're talking about." She snatched her hand back.

"So your mom isn't there?"

"Yes, but that's not your business Tori. I'm trying to protect her from something." Her red lips were spitting words out like fire.

"It is my business it's my mother in law's house. Of all the places to take her you take her there right?" I couldn't believe her.

"That's the only place my father wouldn't think to look. If you only brought me here for this shit. I don't need it ok?" she reached for the door but I grabbed her arm. I needed her to know that her shit ends here today.

"I need you to back the fuck off and disappear. We started enough shit as it is so you need to find somewhere else to take her." I still had a grip on her arm.

"Unless you're planning on making love to me you may want to remove your hands. You are not my father and her mom said its ok." She tried to yank her arm away but I didn't release her. With one smooth motion she climbed on my side of the car, straddling me and started undoing my tie.

"What are you doing?" I asked shocked at how fast she was moving.

"Look, I miss you babe. I know you gotta know that we had something Tori. I can't stop thinking about you and it's driving me crazy that we can't be together." Her words were spoken between kisses on my neck. I rolled my eyes in irritation, this was not what I came here for. I reached for her waist to lift her from on top of me, but she slid my hands to her soft breast.

"Lauren stop ok, move." I spoke, though she used her hands to guide mine in a circulation motion on her tits.

The lady killer involuntarily hardened, he wanted to cloud my better judgment.

"Why would you pick here for us to meet? You know its cause you want me too." She continued talking. Before I could answer, she undid the belt of her jacket to reveal her nakedness underneath. This was not good, I wanted to push her out of the car to tell her she was dead wrong, but my body was waking up and there wasn't much time left before I would give in to my base desire. It was still daylight outside, but the tent on the windows shielded us from the possibility of being seen and the fact that our spot was pretty secluded with virtually no foot traffic. She continued to kiss me all over my face and neck and smiled when she realized how hard I was. Her fingers reached down to grab my hardness before unzipping my pants.

"Tori tell me you don't want it?" she asked while biting my lip softly.

"I don't, now move please." I don't think I was as convincing as I thought I sounded in my head. She continued biting my lip and kissing me on my neck in my favorite spot.

'What the fuck are you doing dude, tell this bitch to move and get out of here NOW! Do it now!' I told myself but my body wouldn't move. Her hands found their way into my pants.

I didn't stop her as she eased down on it and began working it up and down. I laid back and felt the sensation of pleasure wash over my body. I hated that it felt so good, I hated that it got this out of hand.

"You know you miss this, you know you want me." She spoke into my ear softly while moving in circles. I kept my hands to my side and my eyes closed. Her wetness wrapped around me with a familiar intensity. I bit the inside of my lip to keep from moaning. She started bouncing faster and faster, slamming her brown ass down on my dick with a great force. With each stroke I was being brought to climax. I grabbed her by the waist and moved my hips in an upward motion until I felt myself cum inside of her. An image of Misha flooded my mind at the moment of my release, she was holding her hands out to me holding a pen and the divorce paper.

"Shit, DAMN!" I yelled, a mixture of pleasure and guilt wrapped together.

"Did you like that?" she asked like it was nothing to it.

"What the fuck? Lauren we are over, there is no more us and I wasn't supposed to do this right now. I meant what I said about backing off." I pushed her off of me so I could zip my pants.

"Do you know who I am? I am Lauren fucking Michaels. I don't need your ass ok? I wanted you but fuck you Tori, FUCK YOU!" she shouted near my face.

"Get the fuck out of my car. Don't text me no more, don't try to fucking reach me again cause I'm done with your ass." I yelled over top of her long lists of profane names she was now calling me. I leaned over her and opened the door and right before she got out of the car she put her hands on my face and pushed hard.

"You ain't shit Tori and I hope you get what the fuck you deserve." Lauren shouted. Instead of grabbing her by the wrist like I wanted to, I waited for her to slam my car door shut and I sped off.

"Shit, shit, shit. Why didn't you stop her ass?" I punched the steering wheel. This didn't go as planned and now Misha was going to come over and probably smell the guilt all over me.

Unbelievable Stupidity
Lauren

I am pissed that I went over to meet Tori's ass like I thought things could go back to the way they were. I couldn't believe he would treat me that way, especially after all that we went through together. I jumped in my rental so angry I didn't even care to close my rain coat. He isn't the only man on earth, I tried to convince myself that I didn't really care about him, but I did care and that's what has me so messed up right now. I don't know why I care but I do.

"Forget him!" I yelled on the top of my lungs inside of my car. I need a distraction and the way things went last night with Charles I may have it.

Charles was polite, sexy, wealthy and generous, though he tried to cover up the tan line on his ring finger I let him know that I was ok with him being attached. We are both busy individuals and the occasional time spent away from his significant other can be well spent in my arms. We spent most of the night talking business, flirting and exchanging ideas, but with how Tori just treated me I felt like I needed to see him sooner. I raced through the streets in the direction of home. I needed to get dressed and head over to get my mother for a few hours. I needed to see her right away. I'm sure Misha told her all of what happened and she probably was upset with me too. His words kept playing on repeat in my head making me want to scream out in protest.

I closed my jacket before stepping out of my car and unlocking my front door. My glass bottom heels were kicked across the room in anger and I stripped away the only piece of clothing I had on, which was my rain coat.

"I don't know who the fuck he thinks he is, talking to me that way." I ranted to myself all the way to the bathroom to take a shower.

"You don't need him, he's small time anyway. So what he gives it to you good, you can get that from anywhere." My brain wouldn't allow me to relax as I coached myself into feeling better. The warm water streamed from the shower head, hitting my body and erasing remnants of Tori left behind in my unbelievable stupidity. I stayed in the shower longer than usual before stepping out and towel drying. Nothing in my closet spoke to me so I started pulling open drawers until I came across a yellow ankle length maxi sundress. I slipped it over my head and reached for my black sandals.

I dialed over to Misha's mom's house.

"Hello?"

"Hi Ms. Marshall. May I speak to my mother please?" I asked as she answered the phone.

"Sure thing, hold on." I could hear her place the phone on a hard surface and call out to my mother.

"Hello?" My mother's voice spoke through the other end.

"Hi mom. Are you ok?" I asked.

"Yes, I'm fine. They've been very nice. Where are you? Are you ok?" she asked with a hint of concern.

"I'm fine I guess. I'm on my way to get you. I'd like to take you out for dinner." I informed her of my plan.

"Ok, I'll get myself together now then." She said before we ended our call. I grabbed my keys and sent Charles an 'I'm thinking about you' text while walking to my car.

The ride to Misha's moms was a long one. I dreaded running into Misha again. After our last encounter I felt humiliated and now with what just went down with Tori would further make me feel like crap. I hate that she won, I hate that he chose her again. She grew up with a family, brothers who protected her with a vengeance, a mom who spent time with her, gave her affection and advice. Then she had Tori a man who wouldn't let her go even when everything said he should. I pulled in to a park in front of her mom's and her car wasn't there which meant I was safe. I walked quickly up to the house and knocked hard on the door. Her mother answered the he door after the second round of knocks.

"Hello, your mom is on her way out."

"Thanks." I didn't feel comfortable walking in anymore, so I waited on the porch until my mom came out. She wore a white knee length dress with a red rose flower print around the skirt. It framed her curves nicely. She hugged me tightly for a moment and we walked hand in hand to my car. It felt beyond nice, nicer than I could have imagined.

"Where would you like to eat?" I asked her.

"Anywhere is fine honey. I'm just glad we'll get to spend time together." She answered as she locked herself in the seatbelt.

"I have a taste for seafood, if you're ok with that." I started the car and drove in the direction of Memorial Drive. One of my favorite restaurants was Six Feet Under, a four star seafood spot with the best seafood in town.

"Are you ok honey?" she turned in her seat to face me. I wanted to pretend like I was fine, but her eyes baring into my soul prevented me from lying to her.

"I don't know." I kept my eyes on the road ahead.

"Misha's mom told me why she is so mad at you." She gave it to me straight. I couldn't do anything but start to cry.

"Lauren, I want you to know that you're not the only person at fault honey, he had a part in it also. No matter what anybody says about you or that situation I'm still your mother and I'm still hear for you." Her words broke a damn behind my yes releasing a wave of tears behind my tear ducts and I had to pull over in order to prevent an accident. She held me in her arms like a mother holds a child and let me cry until I couldn't cry any longer.

"Thank you. I just want you to know it's not like I started out trying to cheat with my best friend's husband and now I don't have either of them." I spoke through tears.

"Awww honey, I know. Come on let's go eat and we can talk about it a little later ok." She wiped my tears with her fingertips as I straightened back up to drive. It was crazy how life turned upside down. I lost my best friend, my first love, my father, my club temporarily, my car, my sugar daddy, but gained my mother. I'd have to say a pretty fair trade when put into perspective, but it still hurt like hell.

Father Figure
Misha

I drove over to Vivian's house and hit the buzzer for her to buzz me up. Her apartment complex didn't have an elevator so I had to walk up the three flights of stairs. Now I was starting to understand why she might look so good. Her front door was open when I got there.

"Girl, I don't know how you're doing all that." I said while taking a seat on her plush red sofa.

"I'm used to it." She laughed it off. "How are you today?" she asked before locking her door.

"I'm ok, I went looking for apartments today and I'm so irritated that they are all saying I may need a co-signer. My credit is tied into Tori and I don't have any individual credit which is driving me nuts." I huffed.

"I mean if you have the job and the down payment I don't see why it's a big deal. Are you thirsty?" she asked walking into the kitchen.

"Yes, water please." She came back with a bottle of spring water.

"It'll work out don't get discouraged. Have you looked for a few places that don't require a credit check?" she asked seriously.

"Viv, you know those are probably places in the hood and I don't feel like the headache. Enough about me, what about you, how was your day?" I changed the subject.

She told me a few funny stories and not so funny occurrences about her day as a teacher when my phone pinged with a text message. It was from Arnold asking how I was doing. I sent a quick 'I'm fine' message and left it at that. He was becoming a bit too friendly, but I shook it off.

"Let me guess Tori?" she asked.

"No, I was with him earlier. He invited me to lunch." I dodged the question.

"Oh really how was it?"

"Weird I guess, it felt like we were a couple but then it felt like I was just meeting him for the first time. I don't know, we need to get our shit together I know that much."

We continued to talk about me and Tori and she told me about a guy she just met. It wasn't until I looked at my phone again that I realized I was supposed to be back at my mom's before seven cause she had a surprise. I just hoped it wasn't going to be another one of Lauren's relatives moving in.

"Girl, I gotta go, my mom has a surprise that she needs me home for." I stood up and grabbed my purse. Vivian gave me a hug as I walked out of her apartment and back down the stairs to where my car was parked. I dialed Tori's cell. He answered on the fourth ring.

"Hey, were you busy?" I asked.

"Uh, no what's up?" he sounded distracted.

"Nothing, I wanted to let you know that I may not be able to come over, my mom has something at the house she needs me there for."

"Really? You sure you're not just saying that?" he asked a bit irritated.

"No, I'm serious. Besides I don't think you miss me." I said with a smile on my face.

"What? Why you say that?" his voice sounded panicked.

"I was joking. Look I'm about to start driving so I'll call you some other time." I waited for an answer. Something seemed different, but I couldn't put my finger on it.

"Ok, Mish, you're wrong. I do miss you." His voice dropped and I didn't know what to say to that so I said good bye and ended the call.

I couldn't help but think how perfect a night it was for going out dancing. Not too long ago, I would have been texting Lauren telling her to meet me at the front of Club Seduction. I couldn't imagine what my mother had up her sleeve, but I sure hope it involved food, I was starving. I arrived at my mother's house twenty five minutes later. The lights were on in the living room and Jerry's car was parked out front, so I knew he was home. I parked and locked the car on my way to the front door. My key wasn't even needed as the door was already unlocked. I heard talking coming from the kitchen so I dropped my keys and purse on the sofa table by the door and headed in that direction. A tall familiar figure stood near the table. His brown skin, still the color of mocha and his low haircut still faded on the sides.

"Manuel?" I asked in disbelief. My oldest brother turned to face me with his eyes lit up.

"Baby girl!" his deep voice filled the crowded kitchen.

"Hey Mish." Mark and Jerry said in unison.

Manuel's arms wrapped around me and held me tight. He was like a designated father after our dad died. He left for the military right after high school and has been traveling ever since. He only made his way home a few times every few years. To feel my brother holding me brought tears to my eyes. He was the watch dog over the house and I knew that my mom must have told him what happened between me and Tori.

"When did you get here?" I asked between tears. My face buried in his chest.

"A few hours ago. Why you crying?" He asked rubbing my back.

"I don't know it feels like forever and I missed you." I pulled away first.

My brother's no nonsense demeanor was always what kept my other brothers and I in check. We used to call him the enforcer because whenever my mother gave an order it was him who got us to move with little to no hesitation.

"You came right on time Mish too, mommy just took her famous roast outta the oven and I'm ready to get my grub on." Jerry rubbed his hands together making us all laugh.

"He still greedy as hell I see." Manuel joked his voice deeper than I remembered. I hugged my mother and washed my hands before helping her set the table.

After the food was blessed and served Manuel looked at me with a very serious expression.

"So what's been going on with you and Tori?" I cringed at having to reveal details I knew he already knew.

"We are thinking about a divorce." I started.

"I know that much but for what?" he prodded lowering his fork back to his plate.

"He found out about the adoption and he had an affair." I tried to word it in a way that would soften the blow.

"Naw, you're not going to rescue his ass Misha. He was having the affair before he found out about the adoption." Mark spoke up angrily.

"Watch your mouth at my mother's table." Manuel glared in Mark's direction.

"Sorry, sorry mama." He apologized.

"Who did he cheat on you with?" he continued his questioning.

"Lauren." I answered and noticed a spark behind his eye. Tori was about to be in a world of trouble and there was really little I could do about it.

"Your best friend, Lauren?" the base in his voice went deeper.

"Yes." I lowered my gaze.

"Manuel, it's getting late. Your sister is going through a tough time and I would like us all to enjoy your company while we eat. Besides, I made the banana pudding you like so much." My mother interrupted his line of questioning. He smiled but the damage was already done. I shook involuntarily and wanted to run up the stairs to warn Tori, but I couldn't feel my legs.

"I've been asking you for banana pudding forever." Jerry started up again.

"I'll make you your own pan next week." My mother laughed at her youngest son.

After dinner my oldest brother tapped me on my shoulder and told me to follow him on the porch. I walked hesitantly at first, he was livid under his calm demeanor.

"How are you holding up?" His question was a bit more compassionate than before.

"I'm ok, I'm not sure what I want to do." I confessed.

"What about divorce?" Manuel looked curious.

"Yeah, I want my husband and my marriage, but I'm hurt and angry."

"Then let me get one hour with him to myself." A sinister glare was behind his eye that almost scared me. I knew what my brother was capable of and so did Tori. They had a run in right before we got married and Manny promised him that if he ever hurt me there would be hell to pay.

"Please don't try to kill him." I said jokingly but I was dead serious.

"We'll be back. I'm going to take Mark and Jerry with me." He said before walking back into the house. I dialed Tori's number quickly begging him to answer in my head.

"Hey beautiful." He answered.

"Tori, I need you to listen, my brother Manuel is on his way with Mark and Jerry." I spoke quickly. I could hear him scrambling to sit up.

"What? Manuel?" he asked again.

"You heard me, my mom called him here and now he's on his way to you." I actually felt bad for him but secretly wanted my brother to scare him straight.

"Shit, did they leave yet?"

"Yes." I lied.

"It's better if you don't leave the house Tori, just apologize." My brother's came outside like they were planning on burning him to a cross. Mark squeezed my shoulder before walking off the porch toward Manuel's rented Toyota Camry.

"Damn." Tori spoke before I ended the call. My mom stood in the doorway.

"Are they going to pay him a visit?" she asked like she didn't already know.

"I'm going." I couldn't sit back knowing that they were going to try to kill Tori. If I knew anything about my brother Mark, I knew he would feel more pumped up with Manny there and Jerry is a huge instigator. Of all the times I've threatened my husband with my brothers I never seriously intended to have them hurt him. I tried to run by my mother, but she wouldn't let me.

"Misha, maybe it's best if you let Manny handle this for you." She held me by the shoulders. I couldn't believe my mother would even suggest that this was ok.

"Mama, I'm not going to sit back and let them beat him to death ok?" I tried to contain the animosity trying to build up in my voice. She let me go and I went looking for my keys. I couldn't find them on the sofa table I put them on when I came in.

"Mama where are my keys?" I spun around furiously.

She had on her stern face as if she didn't plan on telling me. My blood was beginning to boil.

"Mama I really don't want to be disrespectful, but I need to go to make sure they don't hurt him."

"Your brother asked me not to give them to you and I have to agree." She was seriously not going to let me know where they were.

"Then I'll take a cab." I shouted in desperation.

"You are going to wait till they come back." She said as if I was a little girl who needed to obey. I didn't give a damn what she or any of them had to say he was still my husband and I really didn't think beating Tori was going to make me feel any better about the situation. I started goggling cab companies so I could get a ride over to the house. Something in the pit of my stomach let me know that I would regret it if I didn't go.

Tough Love
Tori

I knew this Friday night would be a long one when Misha called to tell me her brothers were on their way. I really didn't care about Jerry or Mark, but her brother Manuel was cut from a different cloth. Not only was he intimidating, but he was also the guy who taught me a few things about being a man and he even threatened my life if I hurt his sister. I respected him as not only my brother in law but as a man and a father figure. I could have stood my ground a lot better if I hadn't slipped up with Lauren earlier in the day. I changed my clothes into a t-shirt and a pair of basketball shorts. I wasn't sure if they thought they were going to have the element of surprise. A big part of me felt like calling a few my boys in case her two punk ass brothers tried to jump me but I decided against it.

I tried to watch a game but my focus was off, my heart paced thinking about fighting for my life. Jerry's ass didn't fight fair and neither did Mark. Leaving the television on, I stepped outside to make sure there wasn't anything for them to grab when it came down to it. When I felt the coast was clear, I stepped back inside only to see the headlights of a car stop in front of my house. I froze and waited for the inevitable. A few seconds later a forceful knock sounded on my front door. I flexed my muscles one last time and prepared myself for an ambush as I opened the front door.

    Manuel stood center with Mark and Jerry on both sides of him. I did a quick once over to see if any of them had anything in their hands. Manny looked like the man of steel. His 6'3" frame was covered in muscle he gained from the military and years of hard work. I opened the door wide enough to stand inside.

    "Tori." Manny spoke first.

    "Manny." I greeted in return. My heart was pumping adrenaline and nervous energy through my veins.

"Can I talk to you for a minute?" he asked like I really had a choice.

"Sure." I stepped outside. I wasn't letting these niggas in so they could tear my house down.

"So what's this I hear about you cheating on my sister?" he asked much like Misha, straight to the point no chaser. I didn't have an answer cause there really wasn't much to say about it.

"I fucked up and did something unforgiveable but me and your sister both have. We're trying to work things out." I started off.

"Mannnn, just fuck his ass up now." Jerry chimed in over his brother's shoulder.

"Continue." Manuel spoke, ignoring his baby brother's suggestion.

"C'mon what can I say that you would believe? I'm sorry? I know I messed up and that I was way out of line. I never meant to devastate Misha and if I could take the shit back, I woulda never have done it." My irritation with needing to explain my situation to Manny came through my voice.

With no warning Manny grabbed me by my neck and slammed me into the door. His mouth inches away from my ear he started talking.

"What can you say? What can you say? You can be a muthafuckin man about yo shit and tell me that your ass is sorry that you got caught. You can leave my sister alone if your ass don't plan on doing her right. Or you can face the consequences of your got damn actions." I wasn't a kid any more so him gripping me up was not gonna go down like that. I pushed him off me. My force launched him back into his two wanna be goons. Mark lunged forward and swung at my rib cage, but I countered with a punch to his nose. He fell backwards onto the concrete walkway howling like a wolf to the moon. Manny looked calmly at his brother on the ground and back up to me.

"You sure you wanna do this?" he asked like he was about to put me to sleep.

"C'mon man I'm not gonna sit here and let somebody attack me. If you came over here to talk, I'm listening; but if you put your hands on me again, I'm gonna fuck somebody up." I threatened, fully aware that he knew killing techniques I wasn't aware of. Jerry's punk ass tried to push Manny out the way to take a swing but Manny held him back.

"Tori, we both know I will fuck you up." Manny stated.

"Maybe but I'm not gonna lay down and let your ass do it." I pulled my shirt over my head quickly. I knew they could do some damage if they jumped me, but I planned on getting in close to do work on his midsection and using him as a shield when his brothers took a swing. I knew I should have called my boys. Misha's absence spoke volumes, her threats were finally becoming a reality.

"I got this." Manny said to both his brothers. He wiped his hands on his pants before taking another swing catching me in my stomach. I wanted to fall from the blow, but I braced myself and charged forward, holding the back of his head with one hand and punching him in his face repeatedly with the other. His fists moved with precision and speed, landing devastating blows to my midsection. "Fuck him up." Voices screamed from what felt like every direction. I managed to get him off me with a punch to his ear. He stumbled back just enough to shake his head and give me room to land a few punches to his ribs.

He must have been studying mixed martial arts because I felt him lift me by my legs to body slam me on the ground, but I locked my legs and started punching him in his face, powerful blow after powerful blow until he couldn't take the heat and released his grip. I stumbled backwards, tripping over. He charged forward taking advantage of my instability, knocking me to the ground. I held on to him to prevent him from landing any good shots. I could hear both Mark and Jerry yelling for him to beat my ass but I focused. Manny was strong as shit and if I didn't pay attention, I would lose this battle terribly. Somewhere in the distance I heard a car door slam shut and a female voice scream out.

"Manny stop." It was Misha. I was happy she was here, but it gave me just enough strength to kick start my hands into gear. She was shouting at one of her other brothers to get off of her to let her go. I still pulled Manny's torso closer to me until I used one forceful push to knock him backwards and up off of me. He straightened himself quickly and tried to lung forward again but Misha stood in front of him.

"Misha move now!" He barked.

"No." she yelled back. I stood up from the ground ready to go at it again but I knew not to touch her cause that would start a free for all.

"It's alright Misha move." I spoke a bit winded.

"I love you Manny, but I didn't ask you to come here to do this." I knew she was about to start crying because her voice was shaking.

"I'm only going to ask you to move one more time." He warned like when they were kids.

"I'm not moving. So if you plan on hitting him you'll need to hit me first." She stood her ground for the first time in forever with her big brother.

"You're acting like animals out in the street giving my nosey ass neighbors something to talk about. Let's go in the house like civilized people and talk about it." She continued. I kept my eyes on Manny and glanced quickly between the other two. I peeped the use of the words her neighbors like she still lives here.

"Misha move." Manny said again, the fight leaving his voice. I personally didn't want to have a discussion about shit after this; but if it made her happy, I would do it. Mark and Jerry weren't allowed in though.

"Get in the house then." Manny growled in his deep voice.

"Is the door unlocked?" Misha looked back at me.

"Yeah." I answered still trying to catch my breath.

"Manny you go in first." She instructed and surprisingly he followed her orders.

"If you two so much as open your damn mouths I swear I'm kicking you out." She looked at Mark and Jerry. Mark still had his hand over his nose holding it back to stop the bleeding. I bent over to grab my shirt and we all piled into the house one at a time. Before the conversation started I went into the kitchen and grabbed a bag of frozen mixed vegetables to put on Mark's nose.

He caught it grudgingly in midair when I threw it in his direction. The five of us stood around for a moment just staring at each other, nobody sure where to start.

"Two wrongs don't make a right, isn't that what you used to always tell us Manny?" she asked standing in the center of the room.

"Yeah, but that doesn't apply when your husband was caught fucking another woman." He stated sarcastically with his arms crossed over his chest. I flinched at his words more than any of his punches.

"Oh please like I don't know why you and Evelyn are divorced. You're no angel and neither are the two of you." She scanned the room. I started to feel bad that she was trying to defend me when I was really unworthy or deserving of it.

"Misha, I'm your brother, it's my job to protect you from shit like this." He continued.

"I appreciate it, but the reality is I've done some pretty messed up stuff too and I'm not innocent but whipping his ass ain't gone fix the problem now is it?" She reminded me of my sister when she said that.

"All I'm saying is this, he shouldn't have fucked with Lauren knowing she was your best friend and for that I have no respect." Mark chimed in momentarily removing the bag from his nose.

"I don't need every fucking body reminding me okay? I know that but let me deal with it my way." She snapped at her brother. My stomach was starting to hurt and I wanted to lay down.

"I just want, I just need a minute is all I'm." she started crying and I reached my hand out to hold her but Manny pulled her to him first.

I saw the looks of anger at watching their sister cry cross each of their faces, but I hated seeing her cry more than any of them.

"What would you like us to do then?" Manny asked.

"Just give me time to figure things out." She spoke into his chest

"Fine let's go." He pulled away and instructed Mark and Jerry to walk toward the door. He took a moment to get near my face one last time.

"I have you on my radar, and if she comes up hurt again I will kill your ass and it won't be nothing she can do to stop me." I didn't flinch even though I believed he would do it. I knew they had every right to protect their sister, I would have done the same for mine but I wasn't going to act like I was scared of him either.

"Misha?" he stopped at the door.

"I'll be out in a minute." She answered. We both watched as he left the house closing the door behind him.

"I'm sorry." She started.

"It's all good, I expected them sooner actually." I confessed.

"Are you leaving with them?" I asked. I really didn't want her to leave, but I would understand if she did.

"Yeah, I guess. Are you hurt?" she reached out and stroked my chest briefly.

"I'm good. Are you ok is the better question?" I touched her face. Fire blazed through my biceps from Manny's power punches.

"I will be." She lifted on her tip toes and kissed me on the lips. They were soft from her lip gloss. My hands went around her waist and hers around the back of my neck. I love this damn girl.

Playing Catch Up
Lauren

After dinner I decided to treat my mother and I to an overnight hotel stay in Decatur to get far enough away from our current situation. We stopped at a clothing store to pick up sleepwear and changing clothes. She was all smiles saying she felt like Cinderella when her fairy godmother came to fit her for her dress to go to the ball. I was excited to spend some one on one time with her.

"Do you think they sell makeup in here?" I asked. She looked around until she spotted an attendant.

"Excuse me, do you carry any makeup here in the store?" she asked.

"We have a line of mascara and eye pencils and a few nail polishes, but that's about it." The woman politely informed us as we headed in her direction. I picked up a few things and paid for our stuff with one of my credit cards. I still had a few of Arnold's credit cards I'm sure he would cut off soon. But that's ok Charles had heavier pockets and I would soon rise above all of this petty nonsense until I'm back on top again.

    The ride to the hotel was filled with small talk until we pulled into the parking lot of the Courtyard hotel. I told my mom to stay in the car until after I paid and came back out for us to go to our room. We grabbed our shopping bags and headed toward the elevator in the main lobby. My eyes caught site of a familiar handsome face walking my way. It was Ellis Reynolds, a former sugar daddy and self-made millionaire. His custom Italian made suit covered every inch of his well sculpted honey colored body very well. His light brown eyes locked on my face as he approached.

    "Hello Lauren." He stopped a few feet away.

    "Hi Ellis."

    "I see your taste hasn't changed." He smiled. I wanted him to walk away.

"Neither has yours."

"Please forgive me. I'm Ellis Reynolds." He extended his hand to my mother as smooth as silk itself.

"Mom this is an old friend of mine." I introduced them quickly. His eyes were looking over every one of my curves to recall for later no doubt.

"Hi, nice to meet you Mr. Reynolds." She spoke politely.

"Oh there you go honey." A woman's voice came up from behind him. He was momentarily surprised but quickly pulled it together.

"Yes, I'm coming now. Have a nice night ladies." He wrapped his arm around the woman's shoulders and turned them toward the entrance of the bar. The elevator doors opened at the same moment.

"He seems nice." My mother spoke once we were in the elevators.

"Well, sometimes looks can be deceiving." I didn't mean to be sarcastic, but Ellis was a man of a different kind. He was a super freak and although he didn't mind spending money on you, he damn sure made sure he got his money's worth with insane and far-fetched sexual favors. He was a road I wished I hadn't traveled. The girl he was with wasn't his wife either so I knew what he was here to do.

I used the keycard to open our door and we both flopped down on the beds.

"So what would you like to do?" She asked me first as if she were just as excited for us to hang out.

"You want to order dessert and watch a few movies?" I asked. I used to picture doing that with my mom when I was younger. Misha's mom used to invite me over when her and Misha were having a girl's only night and I enjoyed it. I shook that thought out of my mind, I have my own mother now so no need to keep thinking about hers.

"That sounds good. I've always wanted to see that movie Eat, Pray, Love." She sounded excited. I hadn't seen it, but heard great things about it.

"Eat, Pray, Love it is. Can you check over there for a menu?" I pointed toward the small nightstand between the two queen size beds.

While she ordered us an ice cream sundae, I went in the bathroom to change. My eyes were still a bit red from crying earlier, but otherwise I looked pretty good. I slipped the maxi dress over my head and put on the navy blue pajama shorts and tank top quickly. When I came back out, my mom was wearing the pink cotton night gown I bought her.

"I ordered our sundae and it will be coming up soon. Can you believe I was actually able to find the movie on demand?" she informed me. I walked over to my designated bed to get comfortable.

"What are you doing?" she asked.

"Laying down."

"No way, I've been waiting twenty seven years to do this. You're laying here with me." I loved hearing her say that it felt like Christmas when my dad used to surprise me with the biggest, best gifts he could stuff under our oversized tree. I hopped off my bed and snuggled up to my mom as we pressed play with the remote.

A couple minutes into the movie a knock sounded on the door. I moved first to answer.

"I'll get it." I said. A young waiter stood with a cart carrying a tray filled with our sundaes. The table had a few small glass bowls carrying more toppings. I moved out of the way for him to push it through. Before I could close the door, I heard my name.

"Hold up Lauren." I turned to see Ellis walking toward me. I tried hard not to roll my eyes.

"Yes." I answered with attitude. He knew I didn't care for him too much after our last encounter.

"You have a minute?" he asked with a smile on his face. He was so handsome it was almost easy to forget what I didn't like about him.

"You sure your girl isn't going to come flying down the hall on her broom stick?" I asked sarcastically. He laughed while shaking his head.

"You don't have to worry about that. I thought maybe you'd like to connect later." He continued clearly delusional or suffering from memory loss.

"Need I remind you that what I said before still stands? You left me in a room tied up for hours alone Ellis. I'm not interested in your type of fucked up fun." I did air quotes at the word fun. He moved closer to me, attempting to wrap his arms around my waist.

"Awww, you still mad about that? That was an isolated event and I promise it will never happen again." He thought he was smooth, but I only saw him as majorly annoying. His hand forcefully grabbed my ass as the waiter came back through the doors.

"Let me tip you." I yanked away from Ellis embarrassed to have anyone see me like that.

"No ma'am the lady inside already has thanks." The lanky boy walked quickly toward the elevators.

"I have to go Ellis. Let's just let the past stay in the past." I tried to open the door but he grabbed my wrists.

"Ok, ok look Lauren you were one of my best and I miss you. Please consider calling me." He begged. I yanked away and pushed the door open.

"Yeah ok." I closed the door and put all of the locks in place. His ass was surely crazy.

Unresolved Issues
Misha

The ride back to my mom's was a long one. Jerry and Mark continuously praised Manny for how well he fought despite the fact that I was still in the car.

"He just lucky Manny got his ass before I did." Jerry stated. I looked out the window wondering how the hell I got here. On one hand I was happy my brothers were there to defend me, on the other hand it made me feel worse about my situation. Manny sensed my mood and spoke up.

"Change the subject." His voice was serious enough that neither Mark nor Jerry tried to test it.

They began talking about basketball games, players and scores. None of it made a difference to me. When Manny's car pulled up to the house we all piled out of the car and walked toward the house. My mother stood in the doorway and allowed my brothers to go in first.

"Misha let me talk to you for a minute." She stopped me.

"Not tonight please mom. I just want to go to sleep." I looked passed her. I was more than upset I was pissed off.

"I know you're upset, but I need you to understand that Tori will be better for it." She tried to rationalize her behavior and brush it to the side.

"Mom don't."

"Misha." She tried to stop me.

"Mom really don't ok? He is my husband until I sign those papers. He is still my husband and having the life beat out of him is not ever something I want done." My voice went from yelling to hushed throughout that sentence. I didn't want to be disrespectful, but sometimes parents think they can fix your problems or do what's best but mess things up in the meantime. I pushed passed her and lo' and behold my keys were on the sofa table. I grabbed them and walked back out to the car.

"Where are you going?" she asked worried.

"I'll be back." I forced myself to answer.

"Misha wait." She continued to call after me. I didn't stop just got into my car and pulled off. I didn't know where I was going, but I was getting there fast. I pulled out my cell and hit Vivian's number from the call logs. She answered on the second ring.

"Hey Girl, what's up?" her voice came through a bit out of breath.

"Are you busy?" I asked.

"Ah noooo, not really." She panted her answer.

"Are you having sex?" I asked embarrassed. She laughed before she answered.

"Well, kinda but its ok."

"Oh my god, I'm sorry. It's ok I'll call you back." I ended the call before she could respond. My cell phone landed on the passenger seat after I tossed it. I cruised the streets, looking at the familiar houses, neighbors sitting out on their porches. I drove until the houses were no longer familiar. I drove by kids playing under streets lights. I started thinking about my son, I began to picture him as one of those kids riding his bike, wondering what kind of kid he was and if he was really happy.

Tears streamed down my face before I even realized I was crying. At the stop light I lowered my head when a beep jolted my head up. The light was still red so I checked the rearview mirror but no one was there, just a dark night sky. The beep came again and I looked over and it was Arnold smiling like a Cheshire cat on my right hand side in a parked car. Lowering my window I asked.

"Hey, what are you doing around here?"

"I was visiting a friend, are you ok?" he asked sincerely.

"Oh, yeah I'm fine." I wiped my eyes.

"Pull over up there." He used his hand to direct me a few cars up. I pulled over and waited for him to walk up to the car. He walked around to the passenger side and sat down.

"You don't look ok." He stated as if he wanted to cut though the bullshit.

"I will be." I looked down at my hands.

"Look, I'm here right now, unbiased to your situation and I'd like to think you and I are somewhat more than lawyer/client. Tell me what's the problem." He coaxed me with words I wanted to hear but not necessarily from him.

"Everything is wrong, my marriage is falling apart. I don't have my best friend anymore, my brother's tried to kill my husband tonight, and I can't get an apartment without a co-signer because all of my credit is tied up with Tori's and I miss the child I gave up." I didn't stop for air until I was done. Instead of feeling better, I felt worse.

"Ok so take a moment to think about your situation. Your marriage is falling apart, so give yourself time away from him. Your brother's are protecting you it sounds like and you miss your child, so take steps to possibly seeing them again. As far as the co-signer that's not really a problem, I'll help you out with that."

"Why are you being so nice to me? Why are you helping me so much?" I looked at him for answers. A man never helps a woman unless he expects something in return.

"Because I had people lend me a hand to get where I am today, so I know what it's like to need help. I'll pick you up in the morning around nine be ready." He stated before letting himself out of the car. I wasn't sure what he planned on doing.

"But wait, you don't have my address." I spoke through the window.

"I will when you text it to me." He handed me a card with his personal cell number on it. I sat staring at it trying to fight the feeling of going too far that was threatening to creep into my thoughts. Against my better judgment, I sent him the text with the address.

I drove around for another hour before heading back home. I was much calmer when I got there. My mother and brothers were sitting together in the living room watching a movie.

"Hey Mish, you ok?" Manny asked.

"Yes, I'm fine thanks just tired. Goodnight." I walked up the stairs and into my temporary bedroom. For the first time today, I noticed that I haven't seen Ms. Diane all day. Maybe Lauren came up with a solution to her mother's problem. I slipped into my pajamas and under the covers tempted to call Tori to hear his voice before going to sleep. I wondered what he was doing at this moment. I sent him a goodnight text instead. He answered moments later with

                        Goodnight pretty girl,

I more than miss you, I need you

I closed my eyes picturing myself making love to Tori again. I pictured what I would do differently if I could do it all over again. Eventually, I drifted off to sleep, feeling good. I was too far gone to hear my cell phone alarm going off near my head. When it went off again five minutes later I stirred enough to turn it off before remembering Arnold would be on his way. I stretched and shuffled into the bathroom to take a five minute shower. Minutes after I stepped into the shower a hard knock on the bathroom sounded.

"Who is it?" I asked.

"Manny, I need to get in there." He demanded. I knew it was him because no one else was crazy enough to be awake this early.

"I'll be out in a few minutes." I shouted over the water. When I was done I made sure the hall was clear before I stepped out wrapped in a towel to my room.

"Manny I'm out." I spoke in the direction of his old room.

I reached for a pair of skinny leg jeans and a black t-shirt with the word 'Diva' written with sparkling rhinestones across the chest. I had a pair of black wedges to match. After getting dressed I brushed my hair into a messy ponytail and headed downstairs to wait for Arnold. Like clockwork he knocked on the front door at exactly nine wearing a pair of black slacks and a purple dress shirt.

"Prompt, I see." I joked.

"I appreciate you being ready." He answered. We both walked over to his car and he opened my door for me. "So have you already picked out a few places?" he asked.

"Yes, I really like the Briarcliff apartments." I told him.

"What's the address?" he asked. I reached into my purse and pulled out the classified ad with the address on it.

He put the address into his car's gps and headed in the same direction I traveled the day before.

"So tell me something, is this your first place by yourself?" he asked.

"Yeah, I've never lived alone. It's always been my mom's and then when Tori and I got married we lived together."

"Wow, ok. I think everyone should live on their own at least once. It's nothing like it, I miss it actually." He laughed lightheartedly.

Thirty minutes later we were pulling into the parking lot of the Briarcliff apartments. He got out and walked around the car to open my door for me.

"Someone should be here right?" He asked rhetorically. We both walked over to the leasing office and a middle aged red head greeted us.

"Hi, I was here yesterday morning and I filled out an application."

"What's your name?" she started typing something on her computer.

"Misha Carter."

"Ah yes, It says here you will need a co-signer to be approved." Red head stated looking up from the monitor.

"I'm here for that." Arnold spoke up.

"Ok, you will need to fill out a separate application and we will need to run your credit also." She informed him. I thought he would bolt if he knew a credit check was required.

"Not a problem." She handed him a clipboard and we both walked into the lounge area so he could fill out the forms.

The whole process took around two hours after he filled out the form we waited a few minutes to get an answer on his credit. When it came back approved, the woman asked if I had the money to put down. I wrote her a check and she gave me my receipt. They didn't do month to month so I had to sign a six month lease. I had my apartment keys an hour later and was giving Arnold a tour of my very own apartment.

"Wow, it's pretty nice here. Let me know if you need help moving in." He offered.

"Thanks, but I have that covered already. Thank you so much seriously I really appreciate it." I thanked him again I stood in the doorway a moment to long with a huge smile plastered across my face.

Déjà vu

Tori

Misha's sending me that good night text last night made me feel good and terrible at the same time. I had a hard time sleeping and I felt like I went to war with a tank and lost. Everything hurt especially my ribs, I was just glad today was Saturday. What hurt worse was waking up alone. I laid on the couch, flipping through channels finding nothing worth watching. My cell rang around eleven and I looked to see who it was. My boy Cam's number flashed on the screen.

"Yo." I answered.

"Hey man, we're about to shoot some hoops at the court around the corner from your mom's you down?" he asked oblivious to my pain.

"I don't know man." I started.

"Come on man, you can't let the shit going on between you and Misha turn yo ass into a hermit. Get dressed and head over here now." Cam shouted into the phone. Unlike many of my other friends, he didn't have a problem speaking his mind or letting it be known how he felt.

"Alright damn." I hit the end button and forced myself off the couch. Maybe I needed to be around my boys. I was already dressed for the occasion so I grabbed my Jordan's, putting them on by the door, and reached for my wallet and my keys.

I could hear my boys before I could see them. They were shouting profanities back and forth across the court. There were only three of them there so far.

"About time yo' ass made it. I was starting to think you were a figment of my imagination." My boy Tony started in on me.

"Yeah well I'm here now." I hit the lock button on my keys and slid them into my basketball shorts.

"You're on Cam's team since you can't play worth shit." Tony continued. Cam threw me the ball and I tried to pretend I was feeling fine.

"Hey yo, Jason told us about you and Misha dude." Lewis chimed in.

"Good, so now I won't need to talk about it." I took a shot and missed.

Thirty minutes of slamming against my body left me wincing in pain.

"What's wrong with you dude?" Cam asked after we won the first game.

"I got into a fight with Misha's brothers last night." I answered.

"Who Mark or Jerry?" Tony asked with a serious look on his face.

"Naw, though I did make Mark's nose bleed. Manuel's home."

"Whoa!!!" all three of them sang in unison. Manny had a reputation for being a heavy hitter and everyone knew it.

"My bad, shit! Why didn't you call us or something?" Lewis asked.

"Cause they came without too much pre-warning." I confessed sitting with my back against the gate.

"You went toe to toe with Manny, seriously?" Tony asked with a smirk on his face.

"Shut the fuck up Tony, he's a man like the rest of us. I just hope you put the work on him." Cam said in Tony's direction.

"I think I hurt him, but Misha came and broke us up. I really can't stand Jerry's ass though and one of these days I'm going to have to put the work on him too."

"So what? Y'all getting a divorced or just going through a little something?" Cam asked.

"I don't know man. We had a divorce meeting, but nothing is final. I think she wants to give us a try."

"Women need to change their mind a thousand times before they actually make a damned decision." Lewis said shaking his head.

"Well, I'm about to go see my mom real quick." I stood up from the ground, gave each of my boy's a handshake and walked over to the car. I really just wanted to be left alone and all of these questions were making me think about what I wanted to forget.

I drove over to my mom's and sat with her for a few minutes. She made me lunch as she told me all about what nonsense my sister was getting into. After eating and watching an episode of one of her pre-recorded soap operas, I got up to leave.

"You'll be ok son." She hugged me and gave me a kiss on my cheek.

"Thanks mom." I didn't want to head home so I drove in the direction of the movie theatre I decided to catch a movie to get my mind off things.

After finding a parking spot, I jumped out and headed toward the entrance. Walking a few feet ahead was a faintly familiar face, the girl from the bar. She was walking with a light skinned sista with nicely shaped hips. Our eyes caught for a moment before she rolled her eyes with more than a little bit of anger. I felt like I should apologize, but her body language spoke volumes. I couldn't catch a break to save my own life. Everywhere I went there was someone to remind me of how close to a divorce I actually was. I walked over to the bathroom to give her and her girl time to buy their tickets. When I came back, she was there waiting for me.

"Here he is." She said sarcastically. I couldn't help but feel like a case of déjà vu. This reminded me of the time me and Misha met up with Lauren and Arnold at the restaurant and I was waiting angrily for Lauren to come out of the ladies room.

"Do I know you?" I asked like I didn't recognize her.

"Ha! I'm Veronica bitch, but you're right." She glared at me hardcore before walking away with an extra switch in her hips. I decided to leave the theatre I didn't have time for another altercation, especially if her angry ass decided to start some shit.

Moving Day
Misha

I was so excited to actually be moving out of my mom's that I had Arnold drop me off at my mom's and practically skipped into the house. Everyone was downstairs talking in the living room.

"Look what the cat dragged in." Manny spoke with a smile on his face.

"Yes, it's me the woman has just secured her first apartment!"

"Wait, what?" Jerry asked confused.

"You heard me big head, I'm moving out and I need all of you to help me. Not that I have much, but you know what I mean." I informed them. My mother stood up and walked into the kitchen. I knew she was upset, but she would have to get over it.

"That's good Mish take the time to get your head on straight." Manny stood up from the couch and wrapped his arms around me in a brotherly embrace.

"Thank you Manny, now come on and help me pack." I pushed away and started toward the steps.

"Not even a full 24 hours and you're already bossing me around." He laughed as he followed me up.

"Come on Jerry." He shouted over his shoulder.

"I'm coming." Jerry grudgingly answered.

I opened my closet and realized that most of my stuff was already in boxes from when Tori packed them up. I threw most of my shoes on top of a few of the boxes and pointed to which boxes I wanted to go in the trunk and then on the back seat. They both started lifting and transporting all of my boxes. I debated on telling Tori about my move until after I got myself situated. As I walked downstairs, I spotted Eric walking onto the front porch.

"Hey, who's moving?" he asked.

"Me, I'm moving. Why you came to help?" I asked smiling.

"Of course. Where are the boxes?" he asked seriously. I turned around with him following me to my old room.

"You moving far?" he asked

"Not really it's the Viera Briarcliff apartments." I stated.

"Oh really, I heard they were real nice. Okay, is Tori coming with you?" he pried for more information.

"No unfortunately."

"Yeah unfortunately for him." He stepped into my room and lifted one of the heaviest boxes there. It was then that I noticed how sculpted his biceps were. I took a double take.

"When you start working out?" I tried to sound casual, but he laughed anyway.

"For a while now," he straightened up, "Maybe you can come watch me work out one of these days." He offered.

"Maybe." I flirted causing him to stop in his tracks.

"Don't play wit me girl?" he looked my way.

"Maybe you can help get back in shape."

"Tell me when and where and I'll be there." He invited in the same moment Manny came back up.

"Be where?" he asked.

"Wherever she needs me to put these boxes." Eric lied. I bit the inside of my cheek to stop from laughing. When we were done they stood around outside waiting for me to lead them to my new apartment. I walked in the kitchen to say goodbye to my mom.

"Mama I'm leaving." She didn't turn to face me just stood with her back to me at the kitchen sink.

"Mama did you hear me?" I asked.

"Yeah, drive safe." she spoke over her shoulder. I walked up behind her and gave her a hug.

"You're my girl mama and I love being here, but I need my own place to figure my life out."

"I just think you're moving too fast." She whispered.

"Maybe, but I still gotta do it." I kissed her on her cheek and turned to go. My things surprisingly filled up two cars, mine and Manny's rental. Eric insisted he ride with me and Jerry go with Manny.

Once I pulled off, Manny followed and Eric started in on his line of questioning.

"So Misha let me ask you something."

"What?" I answered.

"Why didn't you give me a chance back in the day?" I could feel his eyes on me.

"Because you are my brother's friend and he wouldn't have let us be together anyway." I answered honestly.

"Ok, ok, so it wasn't because you didn't like me or that you didn't think I was attractive?" He continued fishing.

"I always thought you were cute, but it doesn't matter because Mark would try to kill you." I tried to give him a dose of reality.

"But what if I talk to him?" He asked at a red light causing my head to spin in his direction.

"Are you kidding me? I'm not divorced yet and I'm not sure if I want to be. I'm flattered, but I'm not ready to jump into another relationship."

"Ok, fair enough but how about we just hang out for now. I'm a personal trainer by day so that can be our excuse. Just tell me you'll think it over." His offer did sound good, free personal training was priceless.

"I'll think about it." I pulled into the parking lot and waited for my brothers to follow me. I was too excited to contain myself.

It took them two trips to get all of the boxes up into my empty apartment. They walked around and pointed out what they liked about it. Jerry's hating ass mentioned how small the second bedroom closet was. After about an hour, I told them I was going to try to get a bed before it was too late. Eric insisted he go with me, but I turned him down but not before he slipped me his number. I wanted to go with Vivian. She was the best shopping partner and I wanted her to see my new place. I gave her a quick call and she said she was willing to come out. No furniture stores were open on Sunday, so I had to get an air mattress from Walmart. She helped me pick out bathroom décor, dishes, microwave, television, and a comforter set and an air mattress. We sang along with the radio all the way back to my place.

"Oh my goodness girl, this place is gorgeous." She stated after putting the microwave down on the kitchen counter.

"Did you need a co-signer?" she asked while looking around.

"Yeah, I was able to work it out."

"I'm glad. I'm about to be sleeping over your crib from now on." She joked.

"Thanks."

"So did you tell Tori you found a place?" She asked.

"No I didn't, I'll get around to it, but just not today. I start work tomorrow too." We both unpacked the air mattress and began letting it fill up with air. I took her home when it was done. It felt weird driving back to the apartment with no one there to come home to. The apartment came cable ready so I unboxed my new flat screen and connected it to the cable wire and proceeded to watch a movie from on demand. I steered clear of all romance cause it would make me cry about my current predicament and I didn't feel like crying on my move in day.

Almost Back To Normal
Lauren

It's been a few weeks and my mom has been able to go back home. My uncle Joe was released on bail that I paid to make my mom happy. Though he was licensed to carry his gun, he will have a hell of an explanation to make when he gets back to court. My father seemed resigned to the fact that I would never tell him where my mother is and he still has yet to tell me anything about Shannon. It was Friday and Club Seduction was again in full swing. Charles was meeting me there in another hour and I was excited about seeing him again. We've been spending a lot of time together lately making it hard to believe he was actually married.

I looked at the gorgeous black Herve Leger U-neck bandage dress he bought me a few days ago. He told me he wanted to spoil me and that I could have whatever I liked, so I chose the seven hundred dollar dress to test that statement and he didn't flinch. Things were finally getting back to normal and tonight I would celebrate. I stepped into the shower and enjoyed the forceful stream of warm water beating down on my body. I wanted to go back to my life before Tori though I missed him, I had Charles filling in that gap nicely.

My shower lasted thirty minutes before I stepped out and dried off in front of the mirror in my bedroom. I felt a bit bloated and the lower part of my stomach seemed to be protruding a little.

"Spanx it is tonight!" I sang out the words. Tonight would be special because I planned on giving it to Charles for the first time. So looking good in my dress was more than necessary. I went through my routine of applying lotion, spraying perfume, and stepping into my spanx. I pulled the dress over my head before sitting at my vanity to apply my makeup and flat iron my hair. Standing in the mirror to admire my body one last time, I felt like a million bucks.

I sent Charles a quick message asking were we still on for tonight and he replied with a hell yeah, making me laugh. We were going out to eat at Restaurant Eugene's over on Peachtree Rd. I was looking forward to being seen before we headed over to Club Seduction tonight.

I grabbed my keys and my purse before heading out the house. I still loved seeing my new beautiful red Mercedes Benz parked out front. I planned on making a quick stop at my club to check on things before meeting Charles out front. The night seemed electric with all the beautiful people dressed up for a fun night out. Handsome men and beautiful ladies were cruising around in their best clothes. I loved seeing the big crowd already starting to congregate by the front of the club. I beeped at the bouncer standing at the door letting all of the beautiful people in. He gave me a head nod and threw up a hand.

I pulled into my designated parking spot and stepped out feeling on top of the world. Though my office door was closed, the music boomed through the walls. *I need to install sound proof in here,* I thought to myself. I checked the TV monitors displaying each section of the club and saw the people pouring in from the front door, hovering around the bar, and dancing to music in the center of the dance floor. I opened the doors to the office and stepped out into the hallway. A quick wave of nausea hit me, taking me by surprise.

"All of this damn perfume in the air." I choked. I spotted Dom one of the bartenders coming from the bathroom area.

"Hey Dom, can you ask Chris if he can check on the ventilation? It feels a little stuffy out here." I asked.

"Ok, I'll find him now." Dom started walking toward the second level so he could look over the loft to spot Chris.

"I looked down at my cell to check the time and it was about that time for me to head to the front of the club. Charles would be here any minute and the one thing I've learned so far was how punctual he was. Moments later I felt a hand on my lower back causing me to spin around.

"You ok? I ain't mean to scare you" Chris asked with a smile on his face.

"Yeah, I'm fine, it just seems a bit stuffy in here. I felt a sick a few minutes ago. Can you check the ventilation?" I asked. He moved in close and leaned down to whisper in my ear.

"The whole place feels fresh in here lil mama. All the air is working perfectly and I personally feel cool."

"Oh ok, well it might just be me. I'm about to get going ok?"

"When can I spend some more time with you?" Chris asked boldly. Him and I haven't kicked it since my mini crisis a few weeks ago.

"I'll let you know ok?" I lied. I was trying to make my next come up and I needed Charles to help me with that. I headed toward the front of the club and until I reached the door. People were still waiting in line to get in. A few chicks looked beyond ratchet so I leaned over and whispered for my bouncer not to let them in. I couldn't let just anyone come up in my spot or it could start going downhill.

I waited by the curb for Charles' black Mercedes to pull up ignoring a few cat calls from wanna be ballers. Just on time he pulled up and double parked in front of where I was standing. I tried not to lick my lips cause he looked good enough to eat. He stepped out and gave me a long hug before walking me around to the passenger side to let me in.

"You wearing the hell outta that dress." He complimented when we were both settled in the car.

"Thank you handsome. You are looking good enough to taste your damn self." I offered in return. He laughed lightly and took off in the direction of the restaurant.

"Are you looking that good for me?" He asked, glancing at me briefly.

"Of course. How was your day?" I asked. He had a few business meetings earlier today.

"Great actually. I was able to finalize some business and now I feel like unwinding with a beautiful woman and enjoying her company tonight." Charles knew how to make me feel good and that was greatly needed.

"Well, good because I think you'll be pleasantly surprised by this evenings plans." I teased.

"Oh yeah! How surprised?" he asked before placing his hand on my thigh.

"It wouldn't be a surprise if I told you now would it sexy?"

We continued to flirt the entire ride over to the restaurant. Like a gentlemen he open doors, pulled out chairs, and ordered both of us a glass of wine. When we arrived, we were greeted by a very pretty hostess wearing a black evening gown. Her hair was pulled into a swooped bun that made me a bit jealous.

"Your name?" she asked in Charles's direction.

"Johnson, Charles Johnson."

"Perfect, I see you've made your reservation. Follow me please." She grabbed two menus and we walked a short distance behind her to our table for two. The atmosphere was beautiful.

"Your waiter will be with you shortly." The hostess informed us before gliding back to her podium at the front of the restaurant.

"This is really beautiful." I leaned in to tell him.

"I love it here and the food is impeccable. You'll see." He smiled as he looked over the wine menu. A tall, innocently handsome man walked over to the table with perfectly combed blonde hair, sparkling blue eyes, and a smile made for Hollywood.

"My name is Brandon and I will be your waiter for the evening. Would you like something to drink before we get started?" he asked as if he's asked this numerous times before.

"Yes, we'll both have a glass of Pinot Noir red." Charles ordered for us both.

"Thank you sir, I'll be back in a moment." He walked away toward the kitchen area.

"So beautiful, how was your day?" he folded his hands on the table, staring at me with his sexy dark brown eyes.

"My day was fabulous, I got to hang out with my mother today, and my club is thriving again so all is well over here." I answered as the waiter placed our wine glasses before us.

"Are you ready to order?" Brandon asked.

Charles ordered oysters with a peach glaze for us both and took the liberty to order us the most expensive entrée on the menu the beef tenderloin. We talked until the oysters arrived and he held one up to my mouth to feed me. Just the site of the oyster made me feel sick. I excused myself quicky and walked to the ladies room like my ass was on fire.

What is happening? I asked myself. I ran into the bathroom stall and spit up in the toilet. When I was done, I walked over to the sink and looked at myself in the mirror. This was the third time this week I spit up.

Working on Me
Misha

Though I love working for Peter Rosen I was much happier to come home and kick off my heels to relax. My apartment is almost completely decorated and I feel like I have actually accomplished something. Me and Tori have been moving in a positive direction with him meeting me for lunch and actually making a real effort to date me again. He even bought me a silver Altima to get around in. Come to think of it, he and I never really dated when we were younger. It felt good to see him put in the work. We started the process with the Adoption Center to meet with our son and was just waiting for his adoptive parents to get on board with everything. He even changed his cell phone number to show me how serious about fixing us he really was. Tonight we were going to have movie night. He was bringing the movies and a bottle of wine and I was ordering the take out. I had just enough time to take a shower and change into something sexy, but not too tempting.

I was eager to show off some of the results I've been getting at the gym. Eric has been training me for the last few weeks and I lost ten pounds so far. That meant my jeans fit much more comfortably. I had to admit that being in Eric's company helped me to not only see him as my brother's best friend, but as an ambitious man with big dreams. Needless to say, his patience with me is also a tiny bit attractive also. I loved looking at him while we worked out, but I keep that to myself.

I stepped into the shower and let the water pour over parts of my body that has been neglected for a few weeks now. I wanted to practice restraint with Tori, but things were becoming more and more difficult to do, especially with how fine he was. I took a few extra moments to moisturize after I got out of the shower with my Amari scented lotion. He loved this lotion, so I wanted to make him come a little closer. It's crazy how new this all felt. The more we 'date' the more I started to forgive him, but the thought of what he did was always just below the surface threatening to make me unhappy. I was able to see why I fell for him in the first place. His playful nature had a way of making me melt. I heard my doorbell ringing, so I walked garbed only in my panties and bra to the intercom.

"Is that you?" I asked.

"Yes it is Mrs. Carter, can you let me in?" he asked. I buzzed him up, unlocked the front door, and ran back to my bedroom to slip on my form fitting pink satin and lace night gown. There was just enough lace around the bust to be revealing. I heard him enter and sit the bottle of wine on the coffee table. I walked into the living room just in time to see him remove his dress shirt and reveal his muscular body covered in a black wife-beater. He turned around when he caught a whiff of my lotion.

"Damn! You're not playing fair I see." He stated.

"Oh yeah, how's that?" I asked seductively.

"Well let's see, you have on something that begs to be removed. You're also wearing my favorite lotion and if I'm not mistaken, you look a little more toned." He answered while wrapping his arms around me.

"Well, that all speaks fair to me." I kissed him on his lips.

"You can tell though?" I asked after our kiss.

"Tell what?" he loosened his grip and walked over to the couch.

"That I'm more toned?" I answered.

"Yeah, why you've been working out?" he asked uncorking the wine bottle.

"Yeah, Eric's been training me." I stated before taking a seat beside him on the couch.

"Eric who?" he stopped to look at me.

"Mark's friend Eric, he's a trainer." I answered nonchalantly. He sat the alcohol on the coffee table and turned to face me, eyes lit with jealousy.

"You've been training with Eric?"

"Yeah, he offered to train me when I moved in here." I responded

"I bet his ass did. Why you didn't come to me to train you?"

"I don't know, I guess cause we were still very close to the edge of divorce." I remarked.

"I don't want him training you no more. I'm serious Mish. His ass been crushin on you since we were kids and I don't want that nigga thinking he has an in." He looked serious, but I thought it was cute. I really wasn't trying to make him jealous, but I didn't want to have any more secrets between us.

"Well, if you don't want him to train me you'll have to take over." I leaned forward and gave him a big kiss on the lips which he used to grip me up and kiss me passionately. He leaned into me, body against body, and held the back of my head as he kissed me making my lower region moist.

"No, but seriously though where has he been training you?" he asked not letting it go.

"In the gym downstairs." I answered unfazed by his questioning.

"Hold on, that nigga's been coming over here?"

"No, he's been meeting me in the community gym. He trains me and then he leaves."

"Oh hell no, I will kick his ass if he comes here again." He was getting all irritated when I wasn't even looking at Eric like that.

"Ok, it's time for this movie." I stated and adjusted myself on the couch.

"You're mine right?" he asked, dropping his voice. I looked him in the eye and answered.

"For as long *you* are mine." He read my meaning and he couldn't get a clearer answer. I'm not going through the BS again.

We both leaned back and watched our movie with me leaning into him. I missed this, the small stuff that lets you know that you have somebody. Midway through the movie, he poured each of us a glass of wine. His fingertips trailed up from my ankle towards my knee and then over my thigh. I spread my legs in anticipation, my body no longer interested in remaining neutral. I wanted him more than I've wanted him in the past. I needed to feel him inside of me, so I didn't fight his advances, but encouraged them.

"What are you doing?" I asked seductively.

"You'll see." He slid down to his knees and used his feet to push the coffee table away. His lips met my inner thigh, forcing my eyes to close. He kissed upward until he reached the top of my panties. I reached down and placed my hand on the back of his head and pressed him forward. That was all the encouragement he needed to spread my legs and plant kisses on my now, wetness. I moaned with pleasure until he began to slip my panties down.

"You miss me?" He asked between licks.

"Yes!" I answered between moans. While he went to work, I scooted my body to the edge of the couch. Call me considerate as I wanted to make things easier for him. Tori took his time paying very close attention to detail. He knew where to lick and how and it was driving me insane. I reached the couch cushions and squeezed.

Moments later he stood up over me and began unfastening his belt. I sat up and started pulling his wife beater from inside his jeans. With great intensity, we both undressed him until he was fully naked and lifting me from the couch. I wrapped my arms around his neck and my legs around his waist. He held onto me and pushed me down on his hardness. I loved how he felt inside of me, stretching me to fit around him perfectly. Our lips met and we kissed while I rode him standing up. I began to let my hands roam across his back and shoulders. I took for granted how hard his body was and how good he felt against my skin.

Today I wasn't making love to him for him, but for me. I needed what he was giving. I needed to feel special and cared for. I haven't felt that for a while and tonight he was going to work twice as hard to get me where I needed to be. He laid me down on my back and lifted my legs high in the air, stroking me with long, deep strokes. He felt so good my eyes closed without trying.

"Right there." I whispered.

"Right where?" He asked

"Oooh! Right there." I continued to coax him into faster strokes. I opened my eyes to see his chest muscles flex while he moved and held my legs in the air. I couldn't help but reach up and grab his chest. My perfectly brushed hair was now all over the place as he leaned down to kiss me. We moved up and down to the same silent rhythm. Moaning and panting in one another's ear. Tori wrapped his arm around my waist and lifted us both from the couch. He walked me to the bedroom never pulling out of me. The only thing I could think over and over again was *'DAMN!'*

When we arrived in the bedroom instead of him laying me across the bed, he bent me over the dresser and held me by the waist. I wasn't sure where the desire to talk dirty came from, but I started screaming things my mama would be ashamed of. He pounded me with such precision I knew he was a man on a mission. I clawed at my dresser moments before his release.

We continued our love making session for an hour more before getting back to watching television. I eventually ordered Chinese and he went downstairs to pick it up from the lobby. He wasn't supposed to spend the night, but it looked like that was where it was leading.

"So Mish, when are you gonna start working on your community service?" He asked while unpacking the food. I was given sixty hours of community service for the situation with Lauren thanks to Arnold. I didn't have to do any jail time or probation. I think he may have slept with one of the judges or pulled in a favor, but whatever he did I was grateful.

"I don't know I have to look around for a few organizations that are willing to help me out."

"My mom's church always looking for volunteers to help feed the homeless." He mentioned.

"Oh really? That may be too awkward." I don't want to feel uncomfortable surrounded by his mom's church friends.

"I'll do it wit you, how you feel about that?" he joked around, but that may actually be the best option.

"We'll see." I brushed it off. I didn't want to spend more time thinking about it cause it would lead to why I was doing it in the first place.

I lost my appetite thinking about community service and Lauren's dumb ass calling the police when I would have been totally justified in beating her to within an inch of her life. I wondered if Arnold would have still helped me had I really killed her and shook the thought just as fast as I thought it.

"I'm not hungry anymore." I stated.

"Why what's wrong?" he looked worried.

"Nothing, I just don't want to talk about community service and I damn sure don't want to think about why I'm serving it." I snapped.

"Ok, ok my bad for bringing it up just a question." He walked in my direction.

"It's ok maybe you should go."

"C'mon on Misha I wasn't trying to be smart or make you feel bad and we're having a damn good night and I want to be in your company, so again I apologize, but it don't have to go no further than that." He went on making his point so he could stay.

"Fine." I reached for my chow mein and a fork. Cause he really put the work on me earlier.

"You know we're not done right?" He said over a wink. I couldn't help, but laugh.

"I didn't know you ran on batteries." I remarked.

"Yeah well my batteries are self-charging. That little bunny has nothing on me." He said through bites of food.

"Yeah alright, we'll see."

When we were done eating, I checked the time on my cell when I realized I had a missed message. I checked and it was Eric, saying he was thinking about me. I deleted the message and powered down my phone I couldn't risk

Tori seeing it and thinking I had something going on with him. Knowing that he was thinking about me, did make me feel good though.

Little Bundles of Possibilities
Lauren

My romantic night with Charles was cut short after having multiple waves of unexplained nausea. He was understanding though and managed to drop me off at my club. I drove home after promising him I'd reschedule. I was beyond embarrassed even after he let me know he was ok. The whole way home I tried to remember eating something that could have made me sick, but I didn't have anything out of the ordinary. I couldn't reach my condo fast enough. The first thing I did when I got in was dial my mother, which still trips me out.

"Hello?" she answered.

"Mom, I'm not feeling good." I stated.

"Why? What's wrong?" she asked with a hint of worry. It was like I was a little damn girl all over again.

"I keep spitting up and I can't tolerate the smells of certain foods." I started giving her the rundown of my symptoms.

"Are your breasts sore?" she asked. I reached up to press my boobs and they were tender.

"Yes."

"When was your last period?" she asked and I nearly dropped my phone.

"No, no, and no again." I shook my head in disbelief. I couldn't be pregnant. Not now and especially not when things started getting back on track.

"I don't know, oh God please no." I spoke through the phone. This couldn't be happening. I walked toward my bedroom to find my little notebook. I always wrote down when my period came on and went off.

"My period was on." I spoke to no one in particular as I flipped the book to the last page. My heart nearly stopped as I read over seven weeks ago. I was late by almost a month.

"But that's normal right to skip a period right mom?" I panicked.

"Lauren, calm down. It's simple we can get you a pregnancy test." My mom's voice was calm, but I was freaking out. Then it hit me. The last man I slept with was Tori that day in the car. I fell back on my bed with my head spinning. I remembered the day Arnold and I had sex in the hotel when he totally disrespected me and my heart beat sped up.

"Shit! I'm sorry mom. When can we do it?" I asked my mom.

"Come to my house in the morning ok?" she asked.

"Ok, goodnight." I hung up and tossed my phone on the floor. This couldn't be happening, especially not with me. I don't want children because they get in the way of things and I never wanted to be tied down to anyone.

Then I thought about how badly Tori wanted a baby and that Misha's trifling ass couldn't give him one. Maybe this is God's way of putting us together I thought. All I know is that I didn't really know what to do with the possibility of being pregnant. If it was true I could possibly be holding the card to getting Tori back. He would have to consider giving me a chance if I had his baby, right? I stood up and stripped down to my spanx. Then I removed it and walked naked over to my full length mirror. I turned to the side and put my hand to my belly. Having a baby growing inside of me seemed beyond reason and yet I was a bit fascinated with the possibility also. I shook the feeling and walked to my drawer, grabbed a night gown, and slipped it over my head.

It was still early so I walked slowly into my kitchen to get a bowl of my favorite ice cream and to watch a movie. 'What to Expect When You're Expecting' seemed to be a really good movie choice at the moment. I grabbed my throw blanket and cuddled up to watch. Close to the end of the movie, I began to nod off and the television was watching me. I hit the power button and settled in for a night on the couch.

The sunlight hitting my face made me wake up. I stretched and immediately remembered needing to go to my mom's. I was feeling more anxious to know and a lot less scared knowing that if I was pregnant me and Tori might actually have a chance. I walked to the bathroom and turned on the shower water before getting undressed. I walked into my bedroom to grab my phone. I knew what I was about to do may be too soon, but I sent Tori a good morning, we may need to talk text. I know he would be surprised because we haven't talked since the day I stormed out of his car. I didn't wait for an answer just got naked and stepped into my shower. The water felt different today. It felt like a piece of heaven as it slipped between my breasts and down to my stomach. I took a moment to think about everything. After about twenty minutes I stepped out and checked my phone before towel drying and still nothing.

I hit the dial button and called my mom. She answered on the third ring.

"Hey baby." She said.

"I'm getting dressed now and I'll be there in a little bit ok?" I told her before hanging up.

"Ok, I'm already ready so you can just beep your horn." She told me and we both hung up.

I threw on a pair of black yoga pants and a yellow tank top shirt and a pair of black and yellow Nikes' I brushed my hair into a loose ponytail and applied lip gloss and traced my eyes with an eye pencil. I didn't want to go heavy on the makeup when I wasn't sure if I would have a crying spell after the pregnancy test.

I grabbed my keys, wallet and phone, and checked for any messages. The only messages I had were from Charles saying good morning and Chris asking if I wanted to go to breakfast. I sent Chris an 'I'm having breakfast with my mom, but we can do lunch' message and good morning to Charles. I knew Tori was mad at me, but was he mad enough to really ignore my messages. I was upset the entire ride to my mom's house. I beeped the horn and she came to the door a few minutes later. My uncle Joe waved from the doorway. I waved back still feeling a bit weird about the entire situation. She got in the car and gave me a kiss on my cheek. Putting her hand to my forehead as if she could tell if I was pregnant by checking my temperature made me laugh. It was nice having her care about me.

"How do you feel today?" she asked as I headed to the nearest pharmacy.

"Better, I haven't spit up yet, but I'm scared to eat anything while we're out." I told her.

"Well, let's get the test first and then we can rule out other options. I can't tell you how happy I was you called me last night. I told Joe that we may be grandparents." She started laughing. *I'm glad one of us was all in,* I thought to myself. I parked in front of CVS and we both got out. I started to feel a bit claustrophobic the closer we got to the aisle holding pregnancy tests. The walls and shelves seemed to be closing in. I grabbed a few different brands and we walked to the checkout line. I just wanted to get this over with. I hate suspense and would much rather jump to the end of this situation to see the outcome.

A brown skinned, big eyed young man covered in acne scars looked at me with a surprised look when he saw how many tests I put on the counter. I shot him a mind your damn business look and took out my debit card. After paying, I snatched my bag and we both walked back to the car.

"Are you hungry?" I asked my mom. I felt like a really good breakfast.

"Yes actually. Did you want to stop and have breakfast first?" she asked. I nodded yes as we both sat down in the car.

"I feel like waffles and eggs." I could almost taste them.

"That sounds good." She stated. I drove in the direction of West Egg Café. More than eat I wanted to avoid the inevitable.

We were so early there was barely a crowd. I didn't want to be around a lot of people at the moment so that was perfect. After being seated, we both placed our order and my mom asked for a small bowl of fresh fruit sliced. The waitress walked away cherry as ever.

"Who's the child's father?" my mom asked staring me directly in the eye.

"I don't know." I put my head down. I hated having to admit that, especially since I am the first to call a chick a hoe for not knowing who fathered their child.

"Ok, do you have any idea?" Anyone else asking me that question would have provoked a hail storm of curses, but I knew she wasn't trying to embarrass me so I answered.

"Yes, but can we talk about something else. I want to enjoy my food before my life is possibly altered by this situation." She nodded her understanding and we began to talk about meaningless things like the weather and how well my night club was doing.

Our food arrived and it smelled delicious. I didn't gag when I put it to my mouth and was able to get through the entire meal without feeling sick. That was a good sign, when there was nothing left to discuss and our plates were clean my mom insisted on paying for breakfast and we drove back to her house. I took the walk of shame to the bathroom and stared at the boxes before unwrapping a stick and reading the instructions. Simple enough, I just had to pee on the end and wait for it to say positive or negative.

Going wasn't a problem as I didn't go when I left the house. I peed on the stick and placed it on top of the box and came back out of the room without looking.

My mom met me in the hall way and asked if I was ok. I only nodded yes and laid my head on her shoulder.

"C'mon let me check it for you." She pulled away and walked into the bathroom. A happy scream came from within the walls and she came back holding the test with a pink positive sign clearly displayed on the tip. My heart dropped, this was all happening to fast.

"We need to take it again." I told her in disbelief.

"Why, you don't think its right?" she asked.

"To be sure." I answered blankly.

"Ok, well give it another thirty minutes. Did you go to the bathroom before you left the house?" she asked.

"No."

"They say the hormones are stronger in the first urine of the day, but if you want to try again we can wait." I watched her adjust her happiness trying to pace her mood to match mine. I was just confused. I would need to make an appointment with my doctor to confirm. So much of my lifestyle would change and that's if I decided to actually go through with having this baby. I looked down at my phone and still no answer from Tori. I sent him another message and said 'are you still mad?' If he doesn't answer the next best thing is to call him. I wasn't exactly sure what I would say if he answered. With the way things went the last time, I wasn't sure if he would be willing to meet me anywhere.

We went back downstairs and sat in the living room. My mom made me a cup of tea to help me with going again soon. My uncle Joe sat awkwardly watching the news and avoiding eye contact with me. I was curious about him and my dad. I just didn't know how to ask the questions I wanted answers to. It was all strange how two men who grew up in the same house as kids could grow up and be so different. My dad told me that he was going to give me some time to think about things, but he still felt the need to let me know I was only getting half the truth about the situation. I missed the dad I grew up with and wished I could somehow have both my parents without sacrificing one of them. I hated watching the news, but continued to fiend interest until I felt the urge to go again. Then I excused myself and went into the bathroom where the life changing sticks lay waiting for me. I unwrapped a different brand and went again. This time I held it up to watch it change. Just like the first it read a pink plus sign for positive.

"Damn! Now what the fuck are you gonna do?" I asked myself aloud.

My life wouldn't be the same, but maybe just maybe I could still have the only man I gave my heart to on purpose. I would give myself a few more days to find the best approach but no matter what, Tori would have to know.

The Green Eyed Monster
Tori

I would be a liar if I said I wasn't jealous of Eric training Misha, but I played things cool. I didn't want to ruin my chances of sleeping over. Though it felt weird living apart from my wife, I'd take things this way for a short while over losing her completely. I would have to trust that she would stop training with him or I would have to step up my game and meet her after work a few nights a week ready with my workout gear. All I know is that I will check Eric when I see him if he thinks he's going to move in on my lady. It ain't gone happen. I woke up in Misha's bed first. She was still sound asleep, which made me smile. I put in work last night making sure she knew who still owned all of that.

    I went to the bathroom before heading into the kitchen to make breakfast. There was only a carton of eggs, milk, and bread as well as a gallon of her favorite peach tea. I made the best of the situation and made us both fluffy scrambled eggs and toast. Poured two cups of her tea and walked both plates into the bedroom and set them on the dresser before going back to collect the tea. When I arrived in the room again she was sitting up.

"Good morning sleeping beauty." I took her the plate of food and her glass.

"You up being all domestic so early in the morning." She commented with a smile on her face.

"Yeah, well I'm good for more than putting in work." I responded.

"Oh yeah?" She took a bite of her eggs.

"Now tell me those eggs aren't better than yo mama's?" I joked which made her laugh.

"I wouldn't say all that now, but you're a close second." She leaned forward and gave me a kiss. I missed this part of our relationship. I felt like we were on a honeymoon together. She wasn't being standoffish or snapping out on me for wanting attention and I was able to love on her the way I really wanted too.

"What are you doing today?" she asked.

"Well, after I eat breakfast with you, I'm going to take a shower, go on the couch, and watch a few games, have lunch with my lady, and possibly dinner before I go to OUR HOUSE." I emphasized the 'our' so she knew I only thought of this place as real temporary.

"Well, I plan on doing some shopping today, you are free to come along if you like." She continued to eat her food. I really wanted to spend the day inside.

"Well, how long were you planning on being out?" I asked.

"Not really sure I wanted to hit a few stores.' She stated.

"That means one of two things, you plan on being out all day or you're going to be hanging out all day." I tried not to show signs of irritation, but I couldn't help it.

"Tori, I wasn't expecting you to spend the night, but like I said, I only wanted to do a little more shopping for the apartment. You can come with me if you want to, stop being a baby." She tried to play around with me, but a part of me was jealous. She was really acting like she planned to stay here for a while.

"Your ass is gonna have a lot of stuff to pack when you come back home." I stated, not really feeling like eating anything else.

"Awww baby, you feel jealous? Huh? Tell me." She placed her plate on the night stand and leaned over on the bed to kiss me again.

"Stop, now you trying to make me feel like a baby, but I thought we were gonna spend some time together this weekend." I pushed her gently away, but she kept coming until her head rested on my chest.

"We spent time together yesterday, but I'm ok with staying in under one condition." She looked up at me.

"What condition?" I moved my eyebrows up and down like I knew she wanted me to put it on her.

"That you cook both lunch and dinner." She started laughing.

"Get outta here big head, you don't even have food up in here. Now I know why you slimmed down you in here starving yourself." I joked with her.

"Well let's head to the market then." She sat up and passed me my plate as we both finished breakfast.

When we were done eating, I put the dishes in the sink as she went in the bathroom to take a shower. I stripped down to nothing and walked into the bathroom.

"What are you doing?" She asked a little surprised.

"Taking care of my woman." I pushed back the shower curtain and took her by the hand leading her into the shower. I let her stand under the water and watched droplets drip from her nipples like rain. I brought my tongue to her nipple and let the water roll into my mouth.

"You're so nasty." She said softly all the while smiling.

"Not yet, but hold on a minute." I got down on my knees, placing my hands on her hips, and began licking her in her wettest place. She moaned with pleasure holding my head until I felt her knees grow weak.

"You're trying to make me fall." She whispered.

"No I'm trying to make you fly." I spoke between kisses before standing up again. I turned her back to me grateful for nonslip shower mats.

Our shower lasted nearly an hour before we stepped out and got dressed. She joked about not remembering what we were supposed to be doing.

"Whose car are we taking?" I asked

"Yours please." I reached for my keys as she grabbed her purse. Today was back to being a good day and I felt happy again. I headed over to a nearby Publix Super Market and parked the car. We picked out things she would need for the next week and I told her to put her wallet away. I paid for her food and we headed back to her apartment.

"You should really consider breaking that lease and coming home." I said as we were grabbing the bags to take back into the apartment.

"Tori, I'm not breaking the lease, but I love that you want me back home though. Give me a kiss." She pulled me by the shirt over to her. She intended to give me a peck, but I kissed her longer, exploring her mouth with my tongue until we heard the door to the apartment building open. I looked up to see a tall, dark skinned brother step out wearing a pair of black basketball shorts and a tank top shirt. He looked like he might be hitting up the gym regularly too.

"Hey Misha!" He did a quick hand wave.

"Hey Randy." She waved back and tried to walk in the direction of her place.

"Who dat?" I asked.

"One of the neighbors." She answered nonchalantly.

"He ain't tryna holla is he?" I asked. I need to get my wife home as soon as possible. This was starting to bother me. The feeling of not having her to myself was taking a huge toll.

We spent the rest of the day lounging around eating, talking, and me silently sulking about the possibility of my wife losing focus for as long as she is in this apartment.

Divorce Meetings
Misha

The weekend flew by and I must say it left me feeling rejuvenated. It was Tuesday already and Tori and I had another meeting with Arnold today. We were going to discuss dropping the divorce although it was already filed. In the meantime I sat at my desk taking calls from individuals looking to meet with Mr. Rosen. I didn't realize I would enjoy working again as much as I do. I felt important like I was serving a real purpose in society instead of being home reflecting on my miscarriages and how I was going to tell Tori about the adoption.

"Mr. Rosen, Mr. Jensen is on line two." I called into his phone line.

"Thanks put him through." He answered. I patched him through and switched my phone line to the answering service as it was now time to wait for Tori. Arnold said our meeting would be brief. Just to sign a petition stating we would like to postpone our divorce proceedings.

I was standing out front waiting for him to pull up. When I saw his Challenger park a few spots from the door, I walked over as he got out. He kissed me on my forehead before touching my elbow to get to the front door. He opened the office door for me and another woman. I spotted him tense up as she walked through. She slowed down enough to give him an icy stare. I was tempted to tell her arrogant ass that my husband didn't have to hold the door for her. I told him to follow me straight to the conference room where we met previously.

"Are you ok?" I asked when I saw how nervous he looked.

"Yes, I'm fine." He took a seat, but not before looking back at the door again.

"So when do you plan on moving back into the house?" He asked but his question was interrupted by a junior partner carrying a stack of folders.

"How are you?" He asked before taking a seat across from us.

"Fine, thanks." Both Tori and I answered. Arnold was running a little late which wasn't like him. He was almost always on time. Just as I had that thought he came into the room with the same rude woman Tori held the door open for.

"Sorry I'm late, just wanted to let you know I'll be a few minutes more if you don't mind." The woman though arrogant was very beautiful. Her brown skin looked flawless and she was rocking the hell out of her black pencil skirt and pink quarter sleeve wrap shirt cinched at the waist with a skinny black belt. She interrupted Arnold by coughing in the middle of his apology.

"Where is my manners? This is my wife Veronica Blake. Veronica these are my clients. Now if you'll excuse us, I'll be back in a moment." Arnold excused himself escorting his wife out of the office.

"She's a bit rude I see." I whispered into Tori's ear. He only looked at me wide eyed and more nervous.

A Small World After All
Tori

Seeing Veronica moments before entering the law firm took me by surprise. I thought maybe it was coincidental, but when she gave me a look of death my heart nearly caught in my throat. I saw how Misha's face changed as if she wanted to say something. I had to stop myself from passing out. I just hoped Misha didn't see how nervous I was acting, I just wanted this to end quickly so I could get out of here. That was before Arnold's ridiculous ass came in the conference room with the woman I wanted to stay far away from, especially with Misha sitting in the same room. He then introduces her as his wife and I could feel a noose tighten around my neck.

This is a joke right? I asked God. Why did the world have to be so small? Not only was the lingering potential threat associated with Arnold, the man who sought to destroy me, but also the woman married to him.

The palms of my hands began to sweat and I wanted to excuse myself, but Arnold stepped back into the room.

"Ok, so where were we?" He said while sitting down.

"We've decided to postpone the divorce at this time." Misha spoke up first. I studied his face for indicators that he knew about Veronica and me that night at the bar. A night I wished I could take back. He was however his usual ridiculous self.

"Fine, if that's what you want to do just sign right here." He spoke to Misha, using his pen to point to the sections we needed to sign. I signed as quickly as I could and stood up.

"I need the bathroom." I said.

"Here, I'll show you where it is." Misha offered, "Thanks Arnold." She said as we both walked out of the conference room. I couldn't hear Misha talking to me only the sound of my heart beating in my ears and my blood rushing from my face.

Like a nightmare Veronica was talking to the front desk receptionist. She turned to face us and I grabbed Misha's arm quickly and escorted her out of the building not giving Veronica a chance to say anything if she planned on it.

"Are you ok?" She asked with a worried expression.

"Yeah, I just really want to get out of here. You know how I feel about Arnold and this place." I lied.

"Well, I thought you said you needed the bathroom." She looked at me confused.

"I'll just go at home. You still have a half hour left right?" I asked though I already knew.

"Yeah, I'll call you when I get off. I better get back in. Give me a kiss." She leaned in closer to me and pressing her lips on mine.

"Ok baby." I said and walked as calmly to my car as I could. I almost expected Veronica to stop me, but I made it into the car without hearing my name. I started the engine and drove away barely able to breath as I turned the corner.

"Shit! What the hell was that?" I asked myself aloud. I need to either tell Misha what happened or stay out of any potential circle that would involve me seeing Veronica again.

I parked in front of the house and stepped out taking a quick look around before opening my door. A white envelope was sticking out of the mailbox. I grabbed it along with the other mail and opened the door. I skimmed the mail it was all bills, except for the white envelope with the words: *From Lauren,* it read: I know you said you don't want to talk to me anymore, but I really need to talk to you in person. I see you changed your number, so I couldn't call or send you a text. Call me.

I ripped up the letter and threw it in the kitchen trash. After today, I was afraid every woman I attempted to sleep with in my past or thought about having sex with outside of my marriage would reappear somewhere Misha and I happened to be. I sat on the couch and went over that night in the bar. Veronica came on to me and led me into the bathroom and though I didn't have to go behind her I did. We didn't have sex, but I'm pretty sure Misha wouldn't care about that. We were finally back on the same page and she's been attending marriage counseling with me once a week so this could not be a problem for me. Our therapist helped me realize that Lauren's appeal was the fact that she offered things I wanted from my wife. Finally me and Misha are back to loving each other or getting back to that place and I didn't want to lose it or do anything that would take weeks, months or years to repair.

Dr. Appointments
Lauren

After taking both my tests, I made an appointment with my OBGYN. I need to see the doctor so I can make some major decisions. I was getting comfortable with the idea of having Tori's baby. I actually love knowing that I had his seed growing inside of me. I walked into my doctor's office and signed in.

"Hey Miss Michaels." Chloe, his bubbly blonde haired receptionist, sang out her greeting.

"Hello Chloe." I walked over to an available seat in the waiting area and grabbed a Cosmopolitan magazine while I waited. I had a few chicks waiting ahead of me. I read a few articles completely through before I was called to a back room.

"Miss Michael's what bring you here today?" Dr. Gordon asked.

"Well I believe I may be pregnant. I took two home pregnancy tests a few days ago and they both came back positive." I shared.

"When was your last menstrual cycle?" he asked.

"Close to four weeks ago." I responded.

"Ok, I'm gonna need you to pee in this cup for me and we'll get the results and take it from there ok?" He handed me a plastic cup inside a clear see through bag with two sanitation wipes in it. I walked it over to the small bathroom in the room. I made sure I drank a lot of water before coming so I was ready to go in the cup. I came back out and a few minutes later a nurse came in wearing gloves and took it out of the room. I sat in silent anticipation reading the information on the walls like I do every time I come here. Twenty minutes later and still no answers, I began to grow impatient, tempted to go out into the hallway to see what was going on. A few seconds later a soft knock interrupted my thoughts.

"We have the results Miss. Michaels and they came back positive. So you are pregnant." The nurse gave me the news. I wasn't surprised by it, but more like excited. I watched as she picked up a colorful circular chart and started moving it around.

"Right now you're about three and a half weeks along." I tuned her out as I contemplated my future with Tori. If this wasn't enough to get his attention, I didn't know what was. I left the office after rescheduling my first prenatal appointment.

After sitting in the car for a few extra minutes, I wrote Tori a note asking him to call me. When he didn't respond to my text, I called his number to find out that he changed it. I knew he would still be at work when I left my note, but I hoped he would at least consider responding if not I would have to do something drastic like show up at his work and cause a scene.

I called my mom to tell her that it was true.

"Hello?" she answered.

"Mom, it's official, I just left the doctor's office and they say I am pregnant." I spoke semi-excited into the phone. She belted out a happy scream and then I could hear her crying.

"Why are you crying?" I asked knowing I'd be next.

"Because I am just grateful to have the opportunity to share this with you." She sniffled as she spoke.

"You're such a softie. I'm grateful too though. I love you mom. I'll call you when I get back home ok?" I stated before ending our call. Not too long ago calling Misha would have been next on my list, but that wasn't ever going to happen again, especially now that I was carrying Tori's baby.

Twenty minutes later I parked my car in front of Tori's house and tucked the envelope in the mailbox. I made sure it was sticking out enough for him to pay attention and got back in and drove off. I haven't seen

Charles since our last night together and he was growing impatient. I knew I needed to play my cards right at least until I had a sure fire plan set in motion. Until then I would string him along and milk the cow until it no longer produced any milk. Me and my baby will need a few new toys. I laughed at my inside joke before my phone started to ring. It showed Chris' name and number on the screen.

"Hey Chris." I sang out when he picked up.

"What's going on?" He asked right away.

"Nothing much just got some good news?" I stated

"Oh yeah? What kind of good news?" he asked using his sexy voice.

"I'll tell you when the time is right." I teased.

"Oh yeah? Cool so what are you about to do?"

"Nothing actually," I flirted. Today was a good day and I didn't want to spend it alone.

"You want to come over for dinner and a movie?" He asked seriously.

"I don't think that will be a good idea Chris." I responded.

"Why not? I'm not gonna push up on you." His voice was playful.

"Because we still work together." I gave that lame excuse even though it had no more merit because of how great he treated me when I really needed it.

"Cool, hit me up if you change your mind." He stated before he ended the call. Chris was my safe bet, but Tori is really where my heart lies.

House Warming Gifts
Misha

Today was a long day between Tori acting strange and Arnold's wife sniffing around my desk for the last half hour I was happy to get out of there. She looked familiar but I couldn't quite place her face. Eric sent me a quick text saying he is already waiting for me out in front of my apartment complex so we could do our usual workout routine. Tori would be pissed if he knew I was still working out with Eric, but I liked the results I was getting and if I worked out with him we would only end up having sex instead of actually working out.

 I called Tori to let him know I was on my way home. Eric stood on the outside of his car waiting for me to pull up. I ignored the way his face lit up when he saw me.

 "I'm gonna have to change first. I didn't get a chance to do it after work." I said as I got out of the car.

"Take your time, I don't have anywhere else to go." He said reaching for my small black briefcase. "I'll take that for you."

"Thanks" I stated.

"So how was your day?" He asked like he was really interested in knowing.

"It was interesting. Tori and I had to sign a petition to hold off on a divorce." I stated as he opened the door for me.

"You're planning on working things out?" He sounded a bit disappointed.

"We don't want to rush into divorce quickly. We're trying to decide if we're better together or apart." I answered.

We walked into the gym and Eric began to stretch as I grabbed my briefcase and told him I'd be back after I changed. I spoke to one of my neighbors boarding the elevator and looked at the keypad as it hit my floor.

"Excuse me." I eased by an older white man wearing a colorful windbreaker. Every time I walked in the door I felt happy that it was all mine. I love the feeling of having something of my own. I quickly changed into a pair of grey yoga pants and a blue tank top shirt, and slipped on my ankle socks and sneakers. I brushed my hair into a ponytail on my way back out the door. Remembering to grab my keys as I left.

Eric was already doing a few sets on the ab machine when I walked back in.

"You know the routine, hit the treadmill for twenty minutes on an incline to get warmed up." He instructed. I walked over to the machine and got started. A few minutes later he walked over and stood in front of the treadmill.

"I'm about to make you sweat?" He said with a big smile on his face.

"Oh yeah, how do you plan on doing that?" I asked with a raised eyebrow. He pulled his shirt over his head and

I had to admit that his body was chiseled to perfection. Enough to make my internal temperature rise. I began to laugh.

"You see something funny?" He asked looking over both shoulders.

"Yes, I see the little boy that use to puff up his chest when I walked by back in the day." I said as I jogged in place.

"Little boy? What can I do to show you I'm a man?" He said while reducing the speed on my treadmill.

"Eric, you know *we* can't happen, not right now and not like this." I said seriously.

"Why not? Tori's ass had his chance and he blew it. I'm willing to be all in, 100% and you know your brothers will kick my ass if I don't treat you right." He smirked. I was beyond flattered and Lord knows I was tempted because the real truth of the matter is that Eric was attractive, funny, playful and generous, and a gentlemen but it was all of those qualities that reminded me of Tori.

"Ok, let's change the subject please. I appreciate you caring enough about me to try, but I don't want to be unfair to you and I really don't want to put you in the middle of drama." If he kept it up, I would most definitely have to fire him as my trainer.

He reluctantly changed the subject and taught me a few new kickboxing moves that had me sweating and breathing hard. I finished out the routine needing a shower. When we were done, he tossed me my keys. Right when I was ready to wave goodbye he walked up to me and gave me a hug. His arms pulled me into him firmly. Eric held me there for a minute longer than necessary.

"What are you doing?" I whispered by his ear.

"Something I shouldn't," he answered, "Bye Mish" He let me go and walked out of the doors and into the lobby. I felt mixed emotions about his exit. I didn't know if he was saying a permanent good bye or not. I shook the feeling and headed back to my apartment to shower and change my clothes.

My shower lasted all of thirty minutes before I forced myself to step out and towel dry. I heard my door bell ring, but I wasn't expecting anyone. Wrapped in my towel, I walked to the intercom.

"Who is it?" I asked.

"Hey Misha its Arnold." His voice was confident like he thought it was ok to just show up to someone's house unannounced.

"Did I forget to sign something?" I asked to gauge why he was here.

"Uh, no actually I just wanted to drop off a house warming gift. I meant to give it to you sooner, but forgot about it."

"Give me a moment." I walked back into my room and threw on a pair of jeans and a t-shirt and came back to buzz him up. A few minutes later he knocked on the door. I opened it and there he stood in a perfectly fitted custom made black suit with silver pinstripes. His black and silver tie matched perfectly.

"You really didn't have to do this Arnold, you've done enough as it is." I stepped aside to let him in.

"Well, it's no problem. You've been through enough." He stated while looking around the apartment. "You've done a good job decorating." He complimented. "Here you go." He handed me the large box. I sat it on the dining room table. "You can open it now if you'd like. I meant to give it to you a little while ago but since I was headed over to Park 75 to meet a few associates I thought I'd stop by and give it to you."

"Oh ok." I turned to pull the ribbon from the box and removed the lid. A huge gift basket filled with two bottles of wine, Belgian chocolates, crackers and a huge selection of cheeses sat inside.

"Oh wow, this is beautiful, thank you so much." I said over my shoulder. A moment later I felt Arnold standing behind me. He placed his hands on my shoulders.

"You're welcome Misha. I hope you enjoy everything." He was close enough for me to feel his breath on my hair. I was beyond uncomfortable and this was completely inappropriate.

"Thanks again, well I was actually about to grab a bite to eat." I tried to step away from him, but he tightened his grip on my shoulders.

"What's the rush? I have a few moments to spare." Before I knew it, he was leaning down to kiss me on the neck. I jerked forward and spun around to face him.

"Arnold, what are you doing? This is inappropriate and you know it." I spoke a few octaves away from yelling.

"Misha, you know that I'm attracted to you. I thought I expressed that clearly. I've shown you what it would be like if you would be interested in starting something with me. You're beautiful and you should be spoiled and I have the means to take care of you." He started walking toward me. This motherfucka must have me confused with Lauren. I'm not a trick and the only man I'm having sex with to be taken care of put a ring on it.

I backed away until my back was pressed against the dining room wall. Arnold came close and pressed his lips on mine softly, holding my face in place with his hand. "I'm having a really bad day today and I just need you right now." He whispered in my ear.

"Please don't do this ok. We're both married Arnold." I tried to reason with him. I didn't want him to go crazy on me, so I needed to use my common sense to get me out of this situation that or find a way into my knife drawer.

"My wife is a bitch, she doesn't take care of my needs and walks around like I owe her something. You're about to divorce your husband cause he's an ass." He began to laugh hysterically making me think he was high. "Just give it to me one time and we'll be even." He wrapped his hands around my hair and lifted my head up to kiss my neck.

"NO! Arnold get off of me now. Get the fuck off of me and get the hell out." I began to scream unleashing rage. "If you don't let me go I will call the police." I yelled as he sucked hard on my neck while still forcefully holding my hair.

"No you won't because if you do I will remove my name from this apartment and have a chat with my man Peter Rosen." His voice was low and menacing. I pushed him away from me as hard as I could. He barely budged.

"Arnold think about what you're trying to do." I reasoned.

"All of you bitches are just a like. You have no problem taking shit, but have a helluva problem giving it back." He slammed me into the wall causing me to hit the back of my head. The pain brought tears to my eyes.

"I'm gonna let you think on that and when you're ready to connect let me know." He shoved me again and walked toward the front door leaving me confused and hurt. I reached for my cell phone to call Tori. He was the first person to pop in my head and I swear I wanted him to beat the hell out of Arnold.

Murder on My Mind
Tori

My cell began to ring and Misha's picture flashed across the screen.

"Hey babe." I answered

"Tori, I need you to come right now." She was crying into the phone. I jumped up from the couch and hit the power button to turn off the TV.

"What's wrong? Why are you crying?" I asked

"Arnold, he tried to force himself on me." She spoke through tears. I know I didn't just hear her say what I thought I heard.

"He tried to do what? Where is he now?" I asked walking toward the door. I grabbed my car keys and walked outside to the car. "Misha, calm down and talk to me." I tried to get her to calm down so I could fully understand what she said.

"Arnold just stopped by to give me a house warming gift and then he tried to force himself on me."

"Oh really that motherfucka put his hands on you?" The question was rhetorical, but she answered.

"He slammed me against the wall." She continued.

My blood was boiling. "What the fuck you mean he slammed you against a wall? Are you in the house right now? Lock your doors I'm on my way right now." I hung up and hit the gas. He must be trying to provoke me to catch a case because I have murder on the mind and I wouldn't stop until I had his ass gripped up by the throat. The usual thirty minute ride was cut down to twenty. I sped up and ran through yellow lights, barely stopped at stop signs until I parked in the parking lot and jogged around to her doorway, ringing the bell.

"Who is it?" She asked still crying.

"It's me, let me in." I swung the door open after hearing the bell buzz me through. Running up the stairs, I did not have the patience to wait for an elevator. She opened the door after the first knock like she was standing there waiting for me.

"Now what did that nigga do?" I asked while giving her a hug.

"I was taking a shower and he rang the bell saying he had a house warming gift. I let him in and he said he'd like for me to open it right then. When I turned my back, he came up behind me and held my shoulders, but wouldn't let me go when I tried to move." I walked over to the table to look at the gift basket. I wanted to throw it out of the window. "When I asked him to leave and said I'd call the cops he said I wouldn't because he co-signed for the apartment." I shook my head at her last statement.

"Hold the fuck up, he co-signed for this apartment? Misha, what was your ass thinking about?" I yelled at her. This shit was starting to get deep.

"I wouldn't have been able to move out of my mom's without a co-signer." She tried to explain.

"So you asked his ass to do it?" I tried to contain my anger.

"No, I didn't ask him, he offered to do it and I didn't think you would have done it because we just had the whole divorce meeting at the time."

"Oh he offered the shit?" I walked over to the dining room table and grabbed the box holding the basket. I was going to go find his ass and beat the shit out of him with everything in it.

"Where are you going?" Misha started screaming after me.

"I'm gonna go find his ass." I yelled over my shoulder.

"Wait, I think I know where he is!" She yelled out making me stop in my tracks.

"He said he was on his way to Park 75 to meet with friends. I'm coming with you." She stated.

"No you're not, you're going to stay your ass here and wait for me to call you. I'll be back."

"Tori, please don't do anything crazy." She wrapped her arms around my waist.

"We're beyond that, his ass touched my wife." I kissed her forehead and headed to the staircase. I couldn't believe this dude. I knew his ass was grimy when we went out with him and Lauren that day. I could smell it from a mile away.

He wasn't going to get away with hurting my wife though, not today. I jumped back in my car, tossing the box in the passenger seat.

"Go to Park 75." I instructed my gps to take me to the high priced restaurant where Arnold was gonna get his ass beat. I couldn't believe she would even accept that nigga's offer. He knew what he was doing, preying on her vulnerability and shit. A thousand thoughts was running through my head. I came to a screeching halt at a stop sign with two people crossing.

"Watch where you're going!" the lady yelled in my direction.

It felt like they were taking their precious time. I wanted to beep the horn to make them go faster. When they finally moved out of the way, I pulled off with full force on the gas.

"IN 100 FEET TURN RIGHT." the gps instructed. I pushed the gas to make the light so I could turn, but I was too far away to make it. I was going too fast to brake so I hit the turn anyway. I didn't see the truck coming up beside me until the impact hit the back door. For a brief moment time stood still. Shattered glass flew in my face and at the back of my head. I felt the car spinning out of control until I propelled forward slamming my head against the steering wheel with devastating force before the airbag exploded, punching me backwards and knocking me unconscious. I could hear cars screeching to a halt and lots of voices screaming in the distance before I faded out.

The Unthinkable
Misha

It's been more than three hours and Tori hasn't answered his phone yet. I slid into my shoes and grabbed my keys. I was going to drive around the restaurant to see if I could find anything out. I punched the address of Park 75 into my gps and waited for it to start giving me directions. As I began to drive, I prayed that God would spare Tori from going to jail. I didn't need to go through another potential prison scare, especially related to one of Lauren's crazy ass connections and even worse a slick talking lawyer with clout and friends in high places.

As I followed the gps route, I noticed a scene up ahead that made my heart stop. A silver car was turned upside down. It looked like the car was crunched like an accordion. Another SUV was completely totaled from the front end with smoke billowing from the mangled parts.

The closer I got the more the car resembled our Challenger. There was a tow truck parked off to the side with the driver talking to a police. I pulled off to the side and ran up to an available police officer.

"Excuse me, where is the driver of this car?" I pointed at the Challenger.

"Ma'am, we need you to step back." The officer put his arm up trying to push me back.

"That is my husband, where is driver of the car?" I screamed in the officer's face. He wasn't listening as he pushed me back away from the accident.

My phone began to ring with an unfamiliar number. I started to ignore it, but something said answer.

"Hello." I turned my back away from the cop.

"Hello, is this Mrs. Carter?" a female voice called.

"Yes, it is."

"This is Piedmont Hospital. There has been an accident involving your husband Tori Carter. We need you to get here right away ma'am." The woman instructed me to come to the hospital moments before my heart dropped.

For a moment, I felt deaf. I could see life moving around me, but I felt like I was in the matrix. Tori was in an accident and it was my fault for not stopping him. I knew he was angry and was probably not paying attention.

"Ma'am? Are you there?" The woman called me back to reality.

"Yes, I'm here. I'm on my way now." I walked back to my car and headed in the direction of Piedmont Hospital. I fought the urge to cry all over again not wanting to find myself in a hospital bed beside him.

I pulled up to the Piedmont ER and parked close to the entrance. When I arrived, a pretty black nurse sat behind the desk.

"Hi, I'm Misha Carter, my husband Tori Carter was just brought in. He was in a car accident." The words rushed out of my mouth.

"Yes ma'am. We're going to need you to fill out some paperwork first."

"How is he? What's happening to him?" I asked fear gripping my heart. The nurse looked at me with a sympathetic expression.

"I know that you're worried, but I'm going to need you to fill out these forms on his behalf and the doctor will be out to talk with you, ok?" The nurse passed me a clipboard with a few forms on it. I took it with my hands shaking the entire time.

Tears rushed down my face as I went over consent forms for everything from operating to anesthesia. Insurance forms were present and all I could do was fill them out and wait. A few moments after I handed the clipboard to the nurse and a tall balding doctor wearing a white lab coat appeared.

"Are you Mrs. Carter?" he asked.

"Yes." I nodded my head.

"So we performed a cat scan and he suffered a serious blow to his head. He has swelling, which we think is normal under the circumstances. At this time his spine is fine, but we will be keeping a close eye on that. He has a few broken ribs as well, but right now he is in a coma." The doctor spoke to me, but when I heard coma the blood rushed from my face and down to my feet. My ears began to ring.

"A coma?" I sat down in a chair and the doctor reached out to steady my arm.

"He can remain in a coma for a few days or a few weeks, but at this time we can't really tell. I will keep you posted as we get more news." He stated.

"Am I able to see him?" I asked the doctor.

"Sure in a few moments I will have a nurse come out to get you. They are cleaning him up now."

I dialed Tori's mom's number and waited for her to answer. I didn't hear her voice until the fifth ring.

"Hello?" She asked.

"Mama Carter, we're at the Piedmont Hospital. Tori was in a car accident." I spoke through tears.

"What? Lord have mercy. What happened? Is he gonna be alright?" Her questions were coming at me faster than I could answer.

"The doctor said he's in a coma." The words came out above a whisper, followed by a volcanic flow of hot tears.

"A coma? Oh Jesus, my baby. I'm on my way. Piedmont?" She asked again. I confirmed before she hung up and then I called my mother. She answered on the second ring.

"Hello."

"Mama! Tori was in a car accident." I cried into the phone.

"Are you serious? Tell me where you are, I'll have Jerry give me a ride." She screamed into the phone, panic clear in her voice.

I told her what hospital I was in and sat balling my eyes out like they told me he was dead. A short brunette wearing nurse's scrubs approached me.

"Ma'am?" she asked softly. I looked up, not enough energy to answer.

"You can follow me." She said helping me stand. We walked through a corridor and then down a long hallway. It felt like forever before I was led to a brightly lit room. Tori lie lifeless with his eyes closed. He had cuts on his neck and his face was swollen. I cried instantly.

"Can he hear me?" I asked the nurse.

"It's always good for you to talk to him." The nurse stated while passing me a box of tissues from a little desk by his bed.

"I'll leave you two alone now." She turned and left the room. I pulled the chair up to his bed and reached up to touch his hand. For a moment my eyes scanned the tubes and machines he was connected to. They were keeping track of his vital signs.

"I'm sorry Tori, I should have come with you. I should have stopped you. Oh God why did I even tell you?" I laid my head on his hand.

Twenty minutes later Tori's mother and sister came through his room door and moments after them, my mom. His sister Tasha pulled me in for a brief hug, both dropping our differences for a moment to share our mutual pain. We all stood around his bed in a circle, my mom praying to God for healing and a fast recovery. After we all finally settled down they started asking questions starting with his mom.

"How did this happen?" She asked. I felt at a loss for words. I didn't want to tell them all of what happened because it would get blown up faster than a hand grenade.

"They say he was driving really fast." I repeated what I heard one of the police say at the scene of the accident.

"But where was he going?" All eyes were on me as Tasha asked her question. I put my head down and began to cry again. This is was all too much and I didn't need his mom and sister looking at me like it was my fault.

"Let everyone calm down and give her time to process all of this ok?" My mom interjected. They all agreed, but my heart was heavy and I didn't think I could take another blow to my family.

Finding Answers
Lauren

After leaving Tori the note, I rode over to my mom's house where her and Uncle Joe were having lunch. She answered all smiles.

"Joe look whose here." She almost sang the words.

"Hey Lauren." He greeted me.

"Hello."

"We were having lunch, are you hungry?" she asked while walking into the kitchen to grab a plate.

"Sure what are you having?" I asked.

"I made chicken salad. I use onions, green peppers and roasted tomatoes." She answered. It sounded good. I just hope I could eat it without feeling sick to my stomach. She made me a sandwich, cutting it into fours and placed it with a tall glass of ice water on the table.

"How are you feeling?" Joe asked with a warm smile on his face. It was so weird how much my father looked like him.

"I feel good today surprisingly." I sat down to eat, taking small bites to pace myself.

"Good, good so your mama told me you went to see your doctor today." He tried to carry a conversation and I thought that was nice.

"Yes, that's where I'm coming from now. They confirmed my pregnancy." I tried to contain my smile.

"You would swear they told your mother she was pregnant with how happy she's been walking around here." He laughed in between bites of his food. It was amazing how happy they were together, even after all of this time. I couldn't imagine why my father didn't like his brother. Before I realized it, tears were streaming down my face.

"What's the matter Lauren?" My mother asked, standing up.

"Nothing, I'm just happy." I shook my head. This was so unlike me, I am almost never this emotional.

We were able to get through lunch and then we all went into the living room to watch television, but I had a different plan. I needed to understand the man that raised me. I needed some answers.

"Joe, do you mind if I ask you a few questions? I don't mean to be disrespectful or to upset you, but there are things I need to know." I started, studying his face for any signs of irritation.

"Ok, what can I answer for you?" he turned to face me.

"What was my dad like growing up?" I asked. He took a deep breath and chuckled.

"The truth?" He asked.

"Yes please don't hold back."

"For the most part your dad was competitive. He made everything a contest. He hated losing and especially to me. I think it had something to do with our dad and how we were raised. Your grandfather was a piece of work. He would always make up things to see who was faster, stronger and would whip the loser. I was older so there were things I could do better than your father so he caught most of it. After our dad died he kept that contest mess going. I never wanted to compete with him. I didn't see the point in it." Joe finished up and that put some things into perspective. My dad was still competitive in business and within his peer groups.

"What happened that night at the hotel?" I asked even though I knew I might not get an answer.

"When I got to the hotel your dad was already there holding a gun up to a woman and a man. He was screaming at the chick and telling her he should shoot her for cheating on him. I was able to barge in the room because the door wasn't closed completely. I caught everybody off guard and the lady pushed passed me and ran out the room. Your dad aimed his gun at me and I shot him first in his arm. I could have killed him if I really wanted to, but I didn't because he's my brother. I just wanted to threaten his ass for threatening Diane." He finished his side of things. I looked over at my mom who was looking at him intently.

So Shannon made it out alright. That was interesting because a big part of me wanted her to pay for trying to burn me alive in my own club.

"Has he ever apologized for what he did to my mom?" I asked looking back and forth at them both.

"No." They both looked at each other and turned away quickly.

We watched a few reruns of Sanford and Son's and I left after giving my mom a hug. I fought the urge to call my dad and walked to my car. There was still so many questions, but I guess for today I had enough. Though I wanted to be completely happy about being pregnant I felt a big emptiness at not feeling comfortable enough to share it with my dad.

Hope in the Midst of Tragedy
Misha

It's been about two weeks since Tori's car accident. He is still in a coma, but the swelling has gone down some and the doctors are hopeful. I was only given one week leave from work and I had to use it to get things in order with his job. Everyone from his office sent flowers and signed cards wishing him well. He was granted short term disability, so I was able to pay his bills and even felt tempted to break my lease and move back into the house. It was hard going back and forth from the hospital, over to the house to collect the mail, paying bills for both households. I went to the hospital on my lunch break just to spend twenty minutes and then I would come back right after work and spend five hours with him. I read him sports news and gave him updates on his favorite teams. I read scriptures my mom gave me to encourage me more than him.

I was a wreck in every sense of the word. I was constantly worried that he would wake up from the coma and I wouldn't be there. I just left the hospital and decided to drive over to the house to get the mail and I was pleasantly surprised when I saw an envelope from the Adoption Center. I unlocked the door and turned on the lights to read the letter. It read:

Dear Mrs. Carter,

We are very pleased to inform you that the adoptive family has agreed for you to receive visitation with Justin. They say Justin is very excited to see you and looks forward to your time together. Please contact me as soon as you can and we can begin the process of visitation and other correspondence. Talk to you soon, good day

Julie Hornsby

I flopped down on the couch with my heart overflowing. I couldn't believe that they agreed to me seeing our son. I smiled knowing his name was Justin. I wondered how soon we would be able to meet and if it would be supervised visits. I folded the letter up again and went to tuck it back in the envelope, but a small picture was tucked away into the corner. I reached in and pulled out what looked like a school portrait of Justin. He wore a white button down shirt, I put my hand up to my mouth to block how loud I really wanted to cry. He looked just like Tori, a miniature version of my husband. He was so handsome with his smooth brown skin and sparkling brown eyes. He had a million dollar smile the size of Atlanta with just enough humor behind them to see that he was playful. I could tell that he enjoyed laughing because even in this small picture his smile was natural not fake for the camera. I laid back on the couch with the picture up to my heart and both thanked him for being happy about knowing us and apologizing for ever having made that decision in the first place.

When I was finally able to stop crying enough to see straight, I decided to stop by my mom's to share the good news. When I pulled up to her house I could see Jerry's car out front. I knocked on the door and my mom answered.

"Hey mama." I kissed her on the cheek.

"Hey, I wasn't expecting you here tonight. You ok?" she asked while stepping out of the way for me to pass.

"Yeah, I'm good." I smelled something good coming from the kitchen.

"Have you eaten yet?" she asked walking into the kitchen. Jerry was already at the table shoving food down his throat.

"What you make?" I asked setting my purse down and washing my hands.

"I made fried chicken, green beans and mashed potatoes and gravy." She answered. It all sounded delicious and my mom was a beast in the kitchen.

As she set the plate in front of me, I decided to eat first before sharing my news because I didn't want to lose my appetite. Jerry talked about one of his new girlfriends and how he thought she was the one. I tried not to be rude, but I've heard this all before. When I finished my food and cleared away my dishes, I reached into my purse and handed my mom the picture of Justin.

"Who is..." My mother started to ask, but then her words faded as she stared at the face in the photo. Her eyes began to water.

"What? Who is it?" Jerry leaned over to see the picture.

"It's him!" My mom declared. "He looks just like the both of you." She continued.

"His name is Justin." I told them.

"Aww look at little man. He really do look like Tori and he got your big head." Jerry joked. I bit the inside of my lip to prevent me from shedding any more tears. The fact that my brother could see me inside of my son made me want to both cry and smile at the same time.

"Hey good people what y'all up to?" Mark asked from behind me. He walked into the kitchen with Eric following close behind.

"Hey Mark. What's up Eric?" Jerry asked them both. Eric looked at me and smiled softly.

"Hey Mish, mom you know I came to eat." Mark patted me on the back and walked over to kiss my mom on her cheek.

"Eric, you're eating?" My mother asked.

"Yes, ma'am if you'll have me." He answered. My mom made them both a plate.

"What are you up to?" Mark asked in Jerry's direction.

"Misha just showed us little man." He handed Mark the picture and Mark's jaw dropped.

"Is this really him? Awww man Mish, he is so big." Mark cooed over the picture.

"Who is it?" Eric asked. I took the picture from my brother and put it in the envelope and walked toward the door.

"Mama I'm gonna call you later." I shouted over my shoulder.

"Ok be safe." she responded.

As I was closing the front door, I heard Eric yell out my name.

"Hey hold up Misha." He said.

"Yes!" I spun around to look at him.

"Did I say something wrong?" He asked with a serious question mark on his face.

"No, I just have to get going." I lied. I didn't feel like explaining to Eric that I gave my son up for adoption and that I may have a chance to see him again. I turned again to walk toward my car.

"Listen, I didn't mean to upset you. Are you going home?" he asked.

"Yes, it's already dark and I want to get in before it gets really late." I didn't want to tell him that after the incident with Arnold, I have been looking over my shoulder and without Tori there to protect me I feel scared most of the time. Not to mention that if I told my brother's I would be setting them up for a long prison sentence because they would undoubtedly go to jail for murder.

"I can follow you in my car." He offered. I wasn't mad at his persistence. It wasn't a bad idea when I thought about it especially with how dark it was outside.

"What are you going to tell Mark?" I asked as if I might agree.

"I'll tell him something came up and I'll come back to get him later on. Drive your car around the block and wait for a few minutes." He instructed before walking back towards my mom's house. He must really like me because he never turned down an opportunity to eat my mama's cooking. I did what he told me and drove the car around the corner and parked on the corner of the block. I spotted his dark blue Ford Explorer, he beeped twice and led the way back to my house. When he parked in the apartment complex's parking lot, I followed behind him and got out.

"Can I walk you up to the apartment?" He asked, which surprisingly didn't make me feel uncomfortable. It was weird, a part of me viewed Eric as an extension of my brothers, but another part of me was beginning to see him as a close friend. He followed me to the elevators and we stepped into the empty box. I pressed the number two and we were both silent as it went up. He didn't start talking until we were outside of my door.

"You sure you ok?" He asked. I really wasn't ok, but this was my burden to carry and as my mama would say I should do it gracefully.

"Yeah, come in." I unlocked the door and sat my purse on the couch. This was the first time he came in my apartment after it was decorated so he looked around slowly.

"It's nice, you decorated real nice in here."

"Thanks, you thirsty? I would make you something to eat since you sacrificed my mother's dinner, but I only have stuff to make a sandwich." I offered.

"I'll take it." He said while sitting at the dining room table. I walked into the kitchen and began making him a turkey and cheese sandwich and poured him a glass of peach iced tea.

"Here you go." I said while sitting it on the table and taking a seat.

"Thanks, so tell me something are they expecting Tori to wake up?" He asked out of curiosity.

"They really aren't telling me anything new. We just have to wait and see. Don't act like you care." I tried to joke.

"I care about your feelings and I know you care about him, so I don't want anything bad to happen to him if it'll devastate you." He answered making me smile.

"Thanks." We continued to talk until the subject of how Tori got into the accident came up.

"If I tell you something, you have to promise you won't tell anyone. Not even Mark, because I swear I will not talk to you ever again if you do." He leaned forward.

"I swear I won't."

"The day of his accident I called him here because Arnold, the guy who got me the job and also helped co-sign for this apartment, tried to force himself on me. He slammed me against the wall and Tori was driving over to confront him and then had the accident." I confessed. He put his cup back down on the table.

"He did what?" he asked with a very serious voice.

"He tried to rape me so Tori went to go handle it, but got in the accident first." I said it again. With a very calm voice he asked.

"What does this Arnold guy look like?"

"Why?" I didn't need another man killing himself to protect me.

"No I'm just asking." He didn't take his eyes off my face.

"About 6'2" with brown skin, he keeps his hair with a low fade, and he always dresses in tailor made suits. He is the Blake in the Rosen, Marshall and Blake Law firm where I work." I filled him in.

"Thanks." He picked up his sandwich and continued to eat.

"What are you going to do?" I asked not sure if I should have told him.

"You don't need to worry your pretty little head about it baby girl." He stood up and walked his plate to the kitchen sink and rinsed it off before putting it away.

When he walked back to the table, he stood in front of me.

"I'm gonna go now." His sudden readiness to leave let me know he was going to try to find Arnold.

"I'm serious Eric don't tell anyone." I stood up in front of him.

"Oh I won't, I promise you on that." Without warning, he pulled me in for a hug. My body was tense for a moment until I realized he wasn't going to let me go until I reciprocated. I put my arms around his waist and held onto him. This was the first hug I've received since the day at the hospital when I first found out about Tori's accident.

I didn't realize I was crying until Eric asked what was wrong.

"Why you crying?" he asked moving his head back enough to look at my face.

"Nothing." I shook my head. Eric leaned in and pressed his lips against mine and held them there for a second, giving me time to back away. His lips were soft as he started to move them over mine.

I wanted to push him away, but I couldn't fight the feeling I was having. Everything in me knew I was wrong, but I felt almost powerless to stop it. He continued to kiss me until I was holding onto his muscular shoulders and the back of his neck. Inside of my head I was screaming, **Misha what are you doing?** But my body was responding like **Yes you need this!** With one swift motion, Eric lifted me from the floor and I wrapped my legs around his waist. He started walking me toward my bedroom, but I used one hand to stop him from moving forward. My bedroom was sacred and I didn't want to bring him in the same place I made love to my husband.

"No?" He questioned without moving his lips from mine. I shook my head no and continued kissing him while he turned to take me to the couch.

His hands slid under my black dress shirt and he rubbed my skin, taking moments to squeeze me.

"Do you know how long I've waited to make love to you?" He asked through kisses on my shoulder. I really didn't want him to talk to me because it would remind me that he wasn't Tori. I had my eyes closed so I wouldn't look at him.

"I've wanted you, needed you forever." He kept talking and it was killing my vibe, which was a good thing I suppose. His fingers pulled my shirt up and over my head before lying me down on the couch. He stood over me for a moment, looking down seductively as he removed his shirt. I took in all of his tattoo covered chest and biceps for a moment. He looked so good, better than any man should be allowed to look at the moment. Eric lowered himself over top of me and began massaging my breasts with the palms of his hands. Soft kisses were planted against my collarbone and then the tops of my breast.

If I were going to go along with this, I didn't need romance from Eric because Tori gave me all of that. I didn't need time to think about my actions. I grabbed his arms firmly and moaned loud in his ear.

"Take me!" I yelled. He lifted up just enough to read my face and started unzipping his pants. Seconds later his cell phone rang in his pocket. I continued to pull at his zipper and pulling him down over me. I didn't give him a chance to step out of his pants before I was lifting my lower half up to him. The ringing of the phone continued. He took it out to see Mark's number jump across the screen.

"Shit!" He said under his breath.

"Who is it?" I asked.

"Nobody." Eric tried to put the phone back in his pants pocket, but he didn't silence the ringing.

"It's Mark?" I asked quickly coming down from my temporary moment of insanity. Before he could answer, his phone stopped ringing but mine started. I jumped up off the couch and grabbed it out of my purse. It was Mark.

"Oh my goodness, he probably think we're together. Go, leave now." I shooed him with one hand and answered the line.

"Hello?"

"Hey Misha, did you see Eric when he left mom's house?" He asked with a hint of suspicion.

"He came out to ask if he upset me, but then he went back in and I left, why?" I asked casually.

"Cause that nigga left me over mom's house and he's my ride. Alright then, I'm gonna hit him up again." He stated before ending the call. Eric had already zipped his pants and put his shirt back on and was half way out the door. He turned to kiss me one last time before jogging toward the stairs.

"Don't forget to breathe!" I yelled after him. When I closed the door, guilt was there to meet me.

See No Evil
Tori

It was dark in here. I wanted to open my eyes, but I couldn't. I knew I was in the hospital because I could hear the beeping of a machine somewhere beside me. The voices of doctors and nurses talking was also somewhere in the distance. My head hurt, but I couldn't tell anyone. I wasn't sure when I could remember what happened to me, but I knew that no one else knew that I was able to hear anything. Misha came up to the hospital and sat with me for a long time talking about basketball. She gave me scores and replays of some of the games. I could tell she was reading most of it because I could hear the ruffling of a newspaper. She held my hand a lot and cried a few times asking me to stay away from the light. So far there wasn't any bright lights and for that I was grateful. My mom also came up often with my sister. They kept praying over me and my mom wiped my face with a warm cloth. She even asked the doctors how they knew if I was in pain or not.

A few times I wanted to cry from frustration. Inside of my head I was shouting. 'Hey, I'm here you can stop talking about me like I'm dead.' But they kept going about life as usual. The only thing that kept me from having a total breakdown was thinking up ways to hurt Arnold. With nothing but time and empty space all I had was my imagination to keep me company. I thought of many different ways to kill him and how to get rid of his body. I just needed a way to force my body out of this motionless state. I knew the doctors said I was in a coma, but they treated me as if they didn't think I would come out of it anytime soon. I heard them pump unsure answers into the ears of my loved ones, but I was determined to fight this with everything inside of me. I wouldn't remain locked in this internal prison for too much longer.

Rude Awakening
Lauren

In the two weeks since I've left Tori that note he hasn't called or even tried to reach me. I've tried to act like I didn't care, but it bothered me ridiculously. No matter what time of day or night I've stopped by his house he isn't home and I don't know what to think about it. I know he didn't move because I can still see his furniture through the blinds. I fought the urge to think that he took Misha on a trip somewhere and they were off together making up. Her ass doesn't deserve him and God must think so too because he allowed me to get pregnant. Creating new commercials for my club has been keeping me busy as Charles and I are making major power moves. He doesn't like me sleeping in hotels or meeting him in sleazy places so he's rented us our own little getaway in Jonesboro to play house in. I enjoyed his company and even thought I could see why someone would settle down with a man like him. However, all of this pretend made me crave settling down with Tori and starting our own little family. I had a plan today. I decided that I was going to take a trip over to his job to get some answers.

I put on a tight black dress and a pair of fuchsia colored stilettos that matched my clutch purse. My makeup was on point and my hair was curled to perfection. I gave myself a once over glad that I wasn't showing enough to still be able to pull this off. I hopped in my Mercedes and headed in the direction of his work. A car was just pulling out of a parking space a few spots from the door. I stepped out and sashayed my way over to the front door where all eyes were on me.

"How may I help you?" A milky white woman with obnoxiously red lips asked.

"Yes, I'm here to meet with Mr. Carter." I stated matter of factly.

"Mr. Carter?" The woman asked confused then went to look at her computer monitor.

"Mr. Eugene Carter?" She asked again.

"No, Mr. Tori Carter." I gave her Tori's name hoping she would hurry the hell up.

"I'm sorry ma'am Mr. Carter is on medical leave." She responded. Medical leave.

"What does that mean?" I asked more to myself than her, but she answered.

"He was in an accident a few weeks ago." She answered as if I should have already known.

"Thank you." I turned and walked quickly out of the building. An accident? What type of accident? The questions started pouring in faster than I could wrap my mind around the idea.

It was starting to make sense why he didn't answer any of my messages. I knew eventually curiosity would have won him over. I drove over to my club where I could sit in the quiet of my office and research hospitals in the area. I went down the list of hospitals that were closest to his mom's house, his house and his job. Each hospital all said the same thing, they didn't have him there. Then I reached Piedmont Hospital and went through all the prompts to get a receptionist.

"Piedmont Hospital, how may I direct your call?" The voice asked on the other end.

"Yes, I'm looking to see if someone is admitted there." I stated.

"Hold while I transfer you to Patient Relations." She placed me on hold and elevator music filled my ears while I waited.

"Patient Relations." A female voice answered.

"Yes, I'm looking to find out if you have a patient admitted there. His name is Tori Carter." I gave her the information to look him up.

"Hold on a moment." I could hear her fingers punching keys on the computer.

"We do have a Tori Carter admitted."

"Can you tell me when he came in and for what?" I asked the woman on the other end.

"He came in about two weeks ago and he was in a car accident. He's currently in a coma." The woman read off the information with no semblance of emotion and all I felt like doing was throwing the phone across the room.

"A coma? Did you just say he is in a coma?" I asked though I was sure I heard her right.

"Yes ma'am. Family and friends are free to come visit." She went on to give me visiting hours and I hung up. Hot tears began to fall from my eyes. I couldn't believe that he was lying in a coma all this time and I was running around with Charles like nothing was wrong in the world.

"You really need to get ya shit together Lauren." I told myself out loud in between crying. I wrote the address to Piedmont down and stuffed it in my purse. Now all I needed to figure out was how to get up to the hospital when Misha wasn't there if she wasn't already living in his room.

I took a ride over to a floral shop and handpicked an arrangement I wanted them to deliver. My note read Get better or Else. I had them deliver it to the hospital today. My heart was heavy and I no longer wanted to spend time with Charles or anyone else for that matter. I then made the decision to call Arnold. We haven't spoken since the day outside of the hotel, but he never sent me any paperwork stating he removed his name from the club.

"Hello." He answered like he didn't remember me.

"Arnold?" I asked.

"Who is calling please?"

"It's Lauren." I answered annoyed.

"Ah! The infamous Lauren Michaels. What can I do for you?" He asked with an arrogant tone lingering in his voice.

"I wanted a status on you signing over my club to me fully." I answered.

"Lauren, why would I sign over my investment without some type of compensation from you?" He asked.

"Compensation? You must be going mad Arnold if you think I am going to pay you for what is already mine." I couldn't believe his ass.

"It's only half yours my love, which means we are equal partners and if you've forgotten that I'm a lawyer. I don't make deals that I can't legally argue." His answer was so smug, I pictured him leaning over a game of chess planning his next move.

"How much?" I asked into the phone.

"How much what?" he asked in return.

"How much will it take to buy you out?" I answered.

"Who says I want to be bought out? I just want my simple life with you back. I miss you baby and I'm dying to make love to you. You know my wife holds out." He lowered his voice like he thought I would think it was sexy.

"Arnold, we are beyond done ok. You should have thought about all of that before you let your trifling ass sister in law try to burn me alive." I snapped.

"Do you really believe I would have let her do that to you if I knew what she was up to?" He asked.

"Yeah well, you didn't stop her either and how is the hoe anyway?"

"I don't know she's disappeared, nobody's heard from her for a while now. She told my wife she was going away for a while, but anyway back to us. Lauren, I will sign over my half of Seduction if you agree to be with me again." He put it out there and let it linger in the air. I knew I would never give in to his old ass again not now and for as long as I had Tori's baby.

"Go fuck yourself Arnold." I shouted into the phone and hung up. I just need to see Tori so I could feel reassured that things would be ok.

It was time to do the unthinkable, I need to go see my dad. I drove over to his house, taking my time to gather up the words I needed to say to him. One of his cars were parked out front. I parked across the street from his house and noticed that his grass was in desperate need of cutting. There were two newspapers lying in the grass. I tiptoed into the lawn to grab them both trying to avoid the heel of my shoe going deep into the dirt.

Instead of using my key, I knocked twice and waited for him to answer. When he didn't come to the door, I dug around for my keys, now at the bottom of my purse and unlocked the door. All of the curtains were drawn shut and it looked extremely dark.

"DAD!" I yelled out. I didn't hear him answer. "DAD!" I shouted again looking around his house. I could tell that his cleaning lady hasn't been there in a little while and empty take out boxes were everywhere. I walked toward my dad's room where I could hear a television playing in the background. I knocked on the door. "Dad?" I asked while peaking around the door cautiously. I didn't want to catch him in any inappropriate acts. He was lying face down in his bed with the covers on the floor. The television was turned on to a Spanish Novella. I walked to the bed to check his pulse.

"Dad" I nudged him until he moved. He reeked of alcohol and sweat.

"Are you ok?" I asked seeing a half empty bottle of Jack Daniels beneath him.

"Lauren!" He sounded surprised to see me.

"What are you doing dad?" I asked confused. I couldn't believe he was letting himself go. His facial hair was now a miniature beard and his once perfectly cut and faded haircut was in desperate need of a barber.

"Why are you in here like this? You need to open the windows and let some fresh air in." I snatched the bottle of alcohol and walked over to the window to let some air into the room. He squinted his eyes at the sight of light.

"NO, don't open the curtains." He protested.

"Dad this isn't you, where is Mary?" I asked.

"She quit or I fired her, one of those." He flailed his arms in the air as he talked.

"Why would you fire her? Come on get up." I pulled at his arm trying to get him to stand.

"You need to take a bath and get cleaned up. This is unacceptable." I couldn't believe I was lecturing the same man who taught me that having a clean house was one of the keys to seducing your prey.

"I don't want to take a bath, I want to sit here and drown myself with my friend Jack." I knew he was already drunk and I've never seen him quite like this before. I was so overwhelmed I flopped down on the edge of his bed and began to cry.

"Aww, don't cry honey, you're my angel don't cry." He tried to sit up but kept leaning sideways. He reminded me of the drunk guy at the bar, always the last to leave and needed a cab to escort him home.

"What is happening to you dad? To us?" I asked between sobs.

"Joe is what happened. I wanted to protect you from my past and now they've found us." He said.

"What are you talking about?" I wiped at my face.

"I know I was wrong Lauren, I shouldn't have hurt your mother, but she was mine first. Joe couldn't just let me have her." He rambled. He must be confused, my mom said that she was going out with Uncle Joe first.

"What are you talking about dad, mom was Uncle Joe's girl." I stated. He laughed hysterically until his laughter turned to tears.

"Is that what she told you? It figures." He used all his might to lift himself up and slid back until his back was resting against his expresso colored leather headboard.

"It isn't the truth?" I asked growing angry.

"Ha! Your mother and I were going out first until she spotted my brother. Just like everything else, he took her from me. I actually told that bastard to fight me for her. He said he didn't have to because she already said she loved him. Can you believe that shit? I loved your mother and when she came to the house with the nerve to ask me for Joe like I was supposed to be fine with it I told her to come upstairs." He stopped for a moment looking out in space.

"I'm confused." I turned around to face him.

"I'm sorry for doing what I did, but I'm not sorry that I have you. I love you Lauren and I don't apologize for it, do you hear me?" He leaned back and closed his eyes again. Tears streamed down my face, why my mom would lie to me is beyond me. Why would she want me to hate my father?

"Dad, I'm sorry." I stood up and walked to his kitchen and got a large trash bag. I kicked my heels off at his door and started collecting all of the trash lying around. When I got back to his room, I threw away empty alcohol bottles, old pizza boxes, and Chinese food cartons. I made my way to his bathroom and ran the faucet to fill the tub, using enough bubble bath to make bubbles.

"Where is Shannon?" I asked over my shoulder. I knew what Arnold told me, but I needed to know what part my father played in. I could hear my father sobbing and I hated seeing what alcohol and grief did to him.

"She left me. I kicked her out for trying to hurt you. You're all I have in this world." He yelled out.

"Dad, c'mon on get in the tub." I told him once the tub was filled. He stumbled into the bathroom, holding himself up with the wall. I helped him take off his socks and shirt.

"I'm going to wrap this towel around you dad so you can take off your pants and boxers ok?" He nodded his head at me. I put the towel up and turned my head so he could undress. I didn't look again until he was sitting in the tub.

This was all beginning to be too much for me to deal with. A drunk man tells no tales was the only thing I could think about. My mother had a lot of explaining to do and as much as I loved her and wanted her in my life I was not willing to be continuously lied to by either of them.

As it Relates to Guilt
Misha

Going to sleep wasn't easy that night, but what was harder was trying to forget about Eric and how good it felt to be held by someone. I missed the feeling of being with Tori and my happiness about getting to meet Justin was now clouded by my guilt. Like I have done for the past few nights, I called my voicemail and listened to Tori's messages. Some were silly, some were ordinary, and some were freaky, but they all allowed me to hear his voice again. I sent up a prayer to God letting him know that if he let Tori survive and come out of his coma that I would forgive him wholeheartedly because now I knew how close I came to falling into the same trap.

Eventually, I fell asleep and was awakened by my alarm to get up for work. I jumped up and took my shower before getting dressed and dialing Julie on my way out the door.

"Good morning Adoption Center, how may I help you?" Her voice sang out to happy for this hour.

"Good morning Julie, it's Misha Carter. I received your letter in the mail."

"Yes, Mrs. Carter. How are you? So the good news is they did agree for you to meet with him. The visits will be with both adoptive parents present until they decide its ok for you to make the arrangements on your own." She started. My heart started beating really quicky. I had to take deep breaths to calm my breathing down.

"Ok, how soon would we be able to meet?" I asked excitedly.

"Well, it's really up to both you and the family. There is nothing preventing you to make it sooner over later. We can hold a conference call for you to speak with the family and when you both agree on a time it's a go." She answered.

"Well, I'm on my way to work right now, but can we do a conference call around noon today?" I asked.

"Well, I'll email them to see if that time works and if it does I'll call you back." We both agreed and hung up the phone with me feeling on edge. I couldn't believe I was this close to seeing my child, our child.

The morning seemed to drag on forever. Mr. Rosen made me get him coffee numerous times and I had to file away briefs and dig up information he needed from the law library. In spite of all the busy work the clock taunted me by moving slower than normal. I spotted Arnold come into the office, wearing a custom made suit as usual, and glance my way briefly. After learning about Tori's accident, he's backed off a bit and we have a silent mutual agreement not to really speak unless necessary. I am so repulsed by him that I can't see why I was almost tricked by his fake charm and generosity. He was a wolf in sheep's clothing and had the world fooled but me.

As the clock struck 11:55am my cell phone began to buzz with Julie's familiar number. I quickly logged out of my phone and switched it to the answering service. "Hello?" I asked almost out of breath, afraid I may miss the call.

"Misha?" Julie asked.

"Yes!" I responded.

"Ok we have Todd and Megan on the line. If you all can refrain from using last names at this time, Misha as you know they are the Justin's adopted parents and Todd and Megan, Misha is his birth mother." Julie started the introductions. I walked quickly to my car so I could sit within the small space and hear everything.

"Hello." We all said in unison.

"Well, I'll start if I may," Megan chimed in, "We want to say thank you for allowing us to raise Justin. He's such a good boy, he really is a happy child and we appreciate you trusting us to raise him." Megan started to cry which made me want to cry.

"Misha, we've raised him knowing that you are his birth mother and that you loved him so much that you wanted him to have more people love him." Todd spoke up. Tears dropped down to my chest.

"Thank you so much. I just want you guys to know that there are really no words to express my gratitude to you and your family. It was a difficult choice back then, but I'm satisfied knowing that he is taken care of." I stated. Julie stepped in to steer the conversation toward meeting.

"Ok, so as you all are aware, you've come to the agreement that you'd like to set up a meeting for Justin to meet his birth parents."

The rest of the conversation went over the details and that they were ok with meeting this weekend. They thought meeting over the weekend would be a good start and felt that Justin was up for it. I tried to contain all of my excitement and waited until the call ended to let out a scream. The first thing I wanted to do was visit the hospital to tell Tori about it finally being time. I cried like a baby that he wasn't awake to experience it with me. The time had a funny way of speeding up when you didn't want it to and my lunch break was over so I had to go back in and face the rest of my day.

As soon as the clock struck five, I was out the door and in my car. I barely put my purse in the passenger seat before I was on my way to the hospital. I wanted to tell Tori the news and I prayed to God he could hear me. I knew he wanted this day to come more than I did. I parked in the hospital parking lot and went straight to his room. I went through our usual hospital ritual of rubbing his lips with ice chips, then putting on a thin coat of Chap Stick to make sure his lips weren't dry.

"Tori, I have some really good news. Baby, I received a letter from Julie and the Adoption Center and they said they are ok with us meeting him. His name is Justin and we're going to come up on Saturday." I started rambling. "Please Tori, we need you to make it baby. I really miss you and I forgive you. I want to move back in the house and I'll leave my apartment. Tori please come back to me." I couldn't help but cry, but for multiple reasons. Despite my sliding down a slippery slope with Eric, I really missed my husband and want him to come out of this coma completely whole. I cried over getting to see our son, but I wanted Tori to be awake when it happened. I also hated feeling this alone without him.

Mind Over Matter
Tori

I could smell her perfume before I heard her come into the room. I felt her rub my lips with ice and then put something smooth on my lips. I wished I could kiss her and say thank you for being here to take care of me. I listened as she told me about the decision on seeing our son. When I heard his name, I wanted to cry but physically I couldn't. Justin, his name is Justin.

"He looks like you Tori." She said and then I wondered how she knew what he looked like, but then she said they sent her a picture. My heart dropped, desperation began to creep up my chest. I wanted to get out of here! I need to get out of this. I need to see my boy.

"Nurse, Nurse! Come here please." Misha started yelling excitedly.

"Yes, what's the matter?" a female voice asked.

"He is crying, look," Misha said, "What does it mean?" she asked.

"Ma'am sometimes the body releases built up fluid, it doesn't necessarily means he is fully aware of what's happening." The nurse tried to calm her down.

"No! Tori I know you're in there. I know you can hear me. I'm here baby, I'm here. Come back to me please. I need you." She yelled as I heard another nurse enter the room and scrambling.

Please God let me know what I need to do to get out of this. You didn't let me die so there is more for me to do here. Show me please God. I started praying because I couldn't be stuck like this another day not when my son would be here for the first time to see me.

Daddy's Girl
Lauren

Once my dad was all cleaned up and his house was as neat as I was going to get it. I made him a cup of coffee and we sat at the kitchen table to talk.

"You look different." He said after a few sips of coffee.

"Oh yeah! You can tell?" I asked with a hint of excitement. I almost forgot what I came here to tell him in the first place.

"Yeah, what is it?" He asked again studying my face.

"Well, you're going to be a grandfather." I stated. He sat his coffee down slowly before pushing back from the table and walking over to me.

"Really? Are you serious? Oh honey. I can't believe it. When did you find out?" he asked. I melted into my father's arms happy that he was happy.

"I just found out a few days ago. I was coming here to tell you. I don't like being upset with you dad, but we need to figure out a way to live in peace. I want you both in my life, in my child's life. We're family, good, bad or indifferent, we are still family." I spoke into his chest.

"I'm not sure that's possible Lauren. Listen I love you and that will never change, but I can't live in a world where my brother is there. I can't look at your mother and be reminded of what he took from me. Do you know that he knew how I felt about her before he took her?" He moved away from me and back to his seat.

"How long were you and mom together?" I asked.

"Why does that matter? He knew she was with me and he moved in on her and she left without so much as a good bye, I don't want you anymore." He babbled on.

"Dad answer the question please." I gave him a puppy dog look that always worked in the past.

"I took her out once or twice, we spotted my brother and they wouldn't stop looking at each other, then he flirts with her in my face like I was fucking invisible." He answered. I couldn't understand why he was making things so much deeper than they actually were.

"Dad, maybe you need to put it behind you. He really isn't the same guy." I started, but my dad started slamming his hand against the table.

"No, no, no! Not you too. You will not defend him in my house. You are my daughter and I will not allow him to have you too." He shouted. Whatever this was I didn't want to have anything to do with it. I was tired of being tossed in the middle.

"You know what dad, did you ever stop think of how this was affecting me? About how hurt I am to learn that I am a product of rape! I'm the child who was conceived in anger and shame." I couldn't believe he was going to make this all about him. I deserve a damn apology from them both. They were ultimately trying to save me from all of their non-sense.

"If you want to be mad at your brother that's ok, hold on to that, but you will not be mad at me for wanting to know my mother. I am not a child and I will always be your daughter no matter what happens. I am always your daughter, always daddy's girl, but I'm not daddy's 'little' girl anymore."

He looked at me for a long moment before he opened up to answer. I didn't know if I made him angry, but I didn't care anymore. I was about to be someone's mother so acting like a child was no longer an option.

"You're right, I'm sorry for bringing you into my problems. I love you and I don't want to lose you especially not to him. I will respect your wish to know your mama for you and the baby's sake, but please don't ask me to be around either of them because as it stands right now I'm not going to." He kissed me on the head and went to pour himself another cup of coffee.

"Now please tell me the father is not that joker I was going to shoot?" He tried to make that remark seem harmless, but it made me shiver nonetheless. I was already trying to erase the image of my father being a rapist out of my mind so adding murderer wasn't something I was ready for.

Harmless?
Misha

When I saw tears coming from Tori's eyes, I knew he could hear me. I felt at peace knowing that he wasn't so far gone that I couldn't get to him. I was more excited that even if he couldn't be awake with me and Justin that he would be present with us. I left after his physical therapist came to massage his muscles and move his limbs around to prevent bed sores. On my way to the car, I battled if I should just quit my job and leave the apartment. I loved my independence, but I didn't want to stay away from my husband any more. This situation made me realize it and if I were at the hospital all day, I could be there for Tori and it would eliminate any idle time for the devil to be busy trying to use Eric to tempt me.

I checked the entire area around the parking lot to my building before I got out of the car. I was always worried that Arnold was going to reappear and try to do something, especially now that Tori was in the hospital. Instead, I saw Eric sitting on the steps leading into the main office.

"What are you doing here?" I asked looking over my shoulder like I expected Tori to approach any second.

"I came to see you." He stated like it was nothing to it.

"Eric, look yesterday was a mistake, we should have never done anything. I don't want to lead you on or anything." I started, but he interrupted me.

"I know things happened really fast, but I also know that you're starting to like me. I don't expect you to be where I am, but can you at least consider." He looked down at the ground for a moment.

"Eric, Tori is lying in a hospital bed. He needs me now more than any other time. I can't be out here fucking with you because his back is turned." I started to walk in the direction of the entrance. Eric grabbed me gently by the arm.

"Hold up, hold on a minute. I'm not trying to be foul, okay? All I'm saying is that I want to be here for you. I want you to know that I'm here. Me being here for you is harmless." He stated. Why did my eyes have to be opened to him? Before he was just Eric, my brother's best friend, and now he was Eric, a handsome, muscular, sexy man that was trying to tempt me into cheating on my husband who is currently in a coma.

"Eric, you are not harmless honey." I did the signature neck roll to emphasis my point. "I'm going in the house now." I said before turning to walk away.

"I want you to know I'm handling Arnold." He said making me stop in my tracks.

"What do you mean handling him?" I asked.

"The less you know the better. See you around." He turned and got in his car leaving me dumbfounded in the parking lot.

I hurried into the building and up in the elevator. What was he planning on doing? I know what handling him meant in the hood and I didn't need any of it leading back to me. I had enough legal problems at the moment. I was so shaken up I tried to call Eric, but he didn't answer. I was nervous because if I knew my brother Mark I knew he acted first and thought later and I was hoping to God Eric didn't share that mentality. I sent him a text saying I need him to come back to the apartment. I had to stop him from doing something dangerous before it was too late. It would be harmless. I convinced myself though I really wasn't sure. He didn't answer and that made me even more nervous.

I need Tori to wake up so we can get on with our lives because things were starting to get way out of control.

Blame It on My Hormones
Lauren

It's Friday night and my club is expected to be extra crowded tonight. An indie rap artist rented the V.I.P. section and has promoted the club for the evening. So on top of my regular attendants, I expected roughly around an extra three to four hundred people. I hired a few extra bouncers for the evening to make sure everything stays in order. I hated the fact that I can't have a drink cause with all of the stress of my damn family I sure needed one. After my shower, I slipped on a black sequined, knee length, one shoulder party dress and a pair of sparkly black Jimmy Choo heels. I love all of my shoes, but pretty soon I won't be able to wear them.

I grabbed my purse, locked up, and headed toward the car. I was going to try not to think about either of my parents tonight as I haven't had a chance to confront my mom, nor was I sure I really wanted to. The pain of knowing Tori was in the hospital and that I couldn't get to him was bothering me even more than my parental situation. But I had a plan, one I thought would not only help me, but buy me more time alone with Tori. I was going to talk to Chris about it tonight. I jumped in my Mercedes and headed toward Club Seduction. There was nothing like seeing a long line wrapped around the building trying to get into my spot. I loved it every time I saw it. I parked in my usual spot and used my key to get into my office. The office nearly shook with the volume of the music. I put my purse in my desk and locked the drawer. I felt like being free so I decided that no matter what I was going to dance tonight and enjoy myself. I opened the door leading me to the lower level. There were lots of beautiful people out tonight. The women, all clad in skimpy and revealing dresses looked like the covers of magazines. The guys were dressed in their best gear and smelled fresh. I walked over to the bar and asked for a cranberry juice mixed with ginger ale.

I took my drink and headed to the dance floor. Closing my eyes and moving to the music, I twirled around like I was carefree with no worries. I felt a few hands touching my waist, my ass, and my legs. I didn't care, I just kept dancing until it felt like I was floating. I felt a hand pull my arm firmly.

"Lauren, what are you doing?" Chris's voice broke my trance.

"I'm dancing." I answered with a smile on my face.

"You're also bumping into people. Are you ok?" he asked with his hand now wrapped around the small of my back pulling me into him. His chest was so hard it stimulated my lower region.

"I'm fine. I just felt like dancing." I answered as I lay down on his chest.

"Ok, I can see you've had enough to drink." He answered. I laughed because I haven't had anything to drink.

"You want to go in the office? We can people watch on the television monitors." He offered.

"No, today I just want to dance. I'm not crazy, or drunk or even close I only want to feel free." I confessed. He looked at me like I was speaking another language because granted I never took the time to act this free because I wanted to appear picture perfect. I wanted to be envied by people coming in like I had my life all together but damn all that tonight.

"Alright well feel free with your eyes open at least. You were hitting into people and a few motherfuckas copped a few feels." He spoke like a jealous boyfriend. "Fine, you can dance with me if you want." I offered, knowing he'd turn it down. He only shook his head and I walked back to the dance floor, grabbed the hand of a pretty young girl, and pulled her into a dance. She laughed but didn't stop me. We bumped hips, gyrated, and laughed at each other with Chris looking on.

As the night went on, I spotted Arnold walking toward the bar and my heart dropped. I couldn't believe he would come here, but I saw a brown skinned woman holding on to his arm. I turned my back and kept dancing like I didn't see him. There was nothing I cared to discuss with Arnold anyway if it didn't have to do with him signing over his half of the club. When I turned around again, there he was steps away from me with the woman clinging to him like he was God.

"Lauren." He stated my name with a smug smirk on his face.

"Hello" I stopped dancing and looked him straight in the face.

"This is my wife Veronica. I just wanted to show her my investment. Would you mind giving us a quick tour?" He asked like he expected me to play along. This bastard must have me twisted bringing his wife in here like I was just going to take it.

"You can show her around, you've been here quite a bit." I snapped back. His face quickly formed into a frown. Veronica looked back and forth between us, picking up on the tension no doubt.

"I thought you said you just recently invested." She asked.

"Oh no, he's been in and out of here quite often Mrs. Blake." I slowed down and emphasized on the words in and out, so she could catch a clue. Her head snapped in his direction. I smiled coyly.

"So again, you can give her the tour, but my office is off limits." I turned my back on the two of them and continued dancing to the music.

What Arnold thought was meant to play me was turned upside down on his own head. I held the cards and I knew he must have wanted me pretty damn bad if he was willing to use his own wife to make me jealous. Blame it on my hormones, but I damn sure wasn't willing to keep tolerating his bullshit and I couldn't remember why I slowed down to talk to him in the first place.

At the end of the night I pulled Chris to the side and asked him for his help. I wanted to use him to visit Piedmont Hospital. I needed him to pretend that he wanted to visit Tori, but then send me a text to tell me if Misha or any of his other family members were there. My plan was to go early tomorrow so that I could get in and check on him. He seemed upset with me asking, but I really needed it done.

"Lauren, doesn't it seem a little bit risky? You wanna go see this dude and he's married." He asked like he thought it would stop me from wanting to go. I wanted to tell him that I didn't care about his wife because I was his baby mama now.

"Chris, will you do it for me? It's important, I wouldn't ask for your help if I didn't need it." I looked at him seductively. He stood within a few feet of my face. He was hesitant so I leaned forward and kissed him a few inches away from his lips.

"Aww, you want to play dirty. Alright, alright I'll go but first." He pulled me into a kiss and I let his lips linger there for a moment, but pulled away a few seconds later. I liked Chris, but he wasn't Tori and I wanted Tori. I was determined to have him even though he said he didn't want me. This baby was going to change everything.

"Are you cool?" Chris asked as we both walked out the door. We were always the last to leave after counting the money. I put the large blue deposit bag in my car's trunk and got into to my car.

"Yes, I'm fine. Remember don't be late. I'm gonna meet you there around ten thirty, ok?" I asked, making sure he knew the drill.

"I got it ok, talk to you in the morning. Be safe." He kissed my forehead and walked toward his car. I pulled off with a craving for chocolate ice cream, which was odd because I hate the taste of chocolate ice cream.

I found a fast food drive thru and ordered a chocolate milkshake. It tasted like heaven and I pumped Calvin Harris' song, 'Sweet Nothing,' in the car with the sun roof open. My life felt much like this song, fast paced, and a bit out of control. I parked the car and sat there for a few minutes daydreaming about me and Tori loving our child. I wasn't sure why being pregnant provoked the desire to give my child what I lacked growing up, a two parent household. Sure, my dad had lots of girlfriends, but he seldom let me meet any of them unless he thought they had potential. I really only got to spend time with Shannon and she turned out to be the biggest bad example a girl could have.

After I pictured my perfect life I set cell phone alarm clock and stepped out of the car and walked barefoot, shoes in hand to the house. I placed my Jimmy Choo's by the door. I was very tired and slipped out of the dress tossing it on the couch and walked to my bedroom in only panties and bra. The covers felt wonderful as I slipped into my queen size bed and drifted off to sleep.

When the alarm sounded, it felt like I had just closed my eyes. I stretched before jumping up remembering my plan from the night before. I took a quick shower, towel dried, and moisturized before spritzing my Chanel #5 perfume. I wanted to feel pretty, that perfume always did the trick. I slipped on a pair of jeans that already seemed a bit more snug than usual. I slid on a black tank top shirt and my red quarter length red motorcycle jacket. I bought it to match my car. After I put on mascara and eyeliner, I ran the brush through my hair a few times before heading out the door.

In the car I dialed Chris on my cell and waited for him to answer. He waited til the fourth ring.

"Hello?" He asked

"It's me, are you ready?" I asked.

"Yes, I'm on my way there now. I'll text you after I get there." He sounded a bit irritated before he hung up. I didn't care this had to be done, whether he approved or not. I followed my gps to the hospital. I received Chris' text that the coast was clear a few minutes after I parked.

"I walked into the main entrance. There was a security desk with a big, dark skinned guy sitting behind the desk. He looked a little out of place in the very bright white room.

"Good morning ma'am." He greeted me.

"Good morning. I am here to visit a patient. Tori Carter." I stated. He looked down at his computer screen, typed in Tori's name, and gave me the room number and directions on getting there. I walked over to the elevators, nervous at what I would see when I got there.

Chris walked by me when I made it to Tori's floor. His irritation oozed from his body like sweat. I stopped at the service desk to let them know I was there to visit Tori. They gave me the ok and I walked over to this room. There he laid on a hospital bed connected to two machines. He wore a hospital gown, covered with two white blankets up to his waist. Tears filled in the corners of my eyes until they spilled over onto my cheeks. I walked hesitantly into the room, stopping at his bed.

"Oh Tori." I whispered before leaning over to kiss him on the lips.

"I'm so sorry, why are you here?" I asked as if I expected him to answer. I pulled up a chair with my back facing the door. I didn't want to see any of the nurses walking by.

"Do you know that I love you Tori? I can't believe this happened to you." I couldn't stop crying. I hated seeing him in the hospital bed.

Please Don't
Tori

The words 'Damn' filled my ears bringing me out of a sleep stage I was in. It came from a faintly familiar male voice that I couldn't quite put my finger on.

"I don't know what the fuck she sees in you." The voice said before I heard their footsteps leaving the room. I wanted to turn in their direction, to open my eyes to see who it was. I hated not being able to move around, it was driving me mad. Then I heard her voice and I knew who it was the man was talking about. I felt Lauren kiss me and I wanted to yank my head away. Panic grew within my chest. I didn't want her here. I didn't want to listen to her, to smell her, I only wanted my wife here and I was offended that she came, especially since it was her who introduced us to Arnold and he was as good as dead if I came out of this ok. She asked if I knew that she loved me and I yelled inside of myself.

I don't care!!! But of course she couldn't hear me so she kept talking. She wouldn't stop rambling on about her love for me and how she didn't know all this time that I was in the hospital. She confessed to be scared to come, but how Chris her club's bouncer helped her out.

I couldn't believe how loud and clear I heard my own thoughts, but the world was oblivious to my internal turmoil. I wanted to shake Lauren and say, 'Please don't, don't tell me you love me, don't waste your love on me, don't expect me to love you back.' I wanted to tell her, 'Please don't feel sorry for me to take her pity and throw it away.' I wanted to tell her to, 'Please don't confuse my physical weakness as a sign of my heart's weakness. I love my wife and there was nothing that would pull us apart again.' I just needed to get out of this so I could make things right between us again. I had a little boy that wanted to meet me and that gave me hope that me and Misha would be ok.

And His Name is Justin

Misha

I woke up at eight o'clock on Saturday morning I was going to meet Justin and his adopted parents at nine. I took a five minute shower and stood in my closet debating on the most appropriate outfit. I wanted to look responsible and unintimidating. The only thing that jumped out at me was an ankle length black maxi dress that I paired with a gold colored cardigan sweater and matching gold sandals. I pulled my hair into a ponytail and applied makeup. I knew I would cry so I used my waterproof mascara. I made sure to put the large pack of tissues into my purse so I could have them on hand. His family agreed to meet with me first and then to allow Justin to come up to the hospital to see Tori. I was so grateful because I knew it would mean a lot to Tori.

Before leaving the apartment, I called my mom and asked her to pray over me and the situation. I needed a little encouragement because I was scared to death that Justin might not like me once he met me. Kids could be brutally honest and that all by itself was terrifying. I was too nervous to eat so I grabbed both my keys and purse and headed toward the door. It was finally here, the day I have been waiting for over the last eight years. The drive to the park was gruesome, I grew more anxious the closer I got and had to talk myself into calming down several times before I arrived. When my car pulled into a parking space just outside of the entrance, I checked my makeup inside of the rearview mirror once more and stepped out. I saw a few people out walking their dog and then my eyes rested on them. I stood still a moment and just watched them altogether. Megan looked about 5'6" with dark brown hair, a very slim woman, and her skin looked recently tanned. Todd was a tall guy around 6'3" with sandy blond hair.

My world stood still when my eyes fell on Justin. He was a tall eight year old. He took after Tori. His brown skin looked milk chocolate, but his smile was what melted my heart. He had the smile of an angel. He spotted me first. Julie suggested I send him a picture when I first asked to see him. He stopped kicking the soccer ball he was running after with Todd and pointed in my direction. They all turned to look at me and my legs involuntarily pushed me forward. I walked up to them and stopped a few feet from Justin. He ran up to me and held out his hand.

"Hello, my name is Justin!" He smiled at me like he's known me his entire life. I reached for his hand trying hard not to drop to my knees and hug him to death.

"Hello Justin, I'm Misha." I said.

"I know your name, c'mon you wanna play soccer?" He pulled me by the hand and led me to where the ball sat in grass waiting to be kicked. Despite my desire to cry, I laughed. He was eager to include me in something he enjoyed.

"Justin, let's play soccer later." Megan chimed in, but I quickly turned to her and said it was ok. I wasn't dressed for soccer, but I would be damned if I didn't kick that ball around for a few minutes. He got the best of me as he maneuvered the ball away from me. Todd played with us until Justin scored a few points and Todd lifted him on his shoulders chanting he was the best.

After our quick game of soccer, I gave both Megan and Todd a hug and asked if Justin and I could walk a lap around the park with them following a bit behind. They both agreed.

"Justin, you're so big." I said as we started to walk. He held my hand.

"My dad says I'll probably be tall like him." He answered. I started to wonder if he really knew who I was or if he was too young to really understand.

"I think so Tori, your blood father is pretty tall too." I answered.

"You're pretty," he stated.

"Oh yeah! Well you're cute." I responded bending down to give him a hug and kiss on his cheek.

"So how do you like school?" I asked, fully content to just be walking with him.

"It's ok. I like playing soccer more than doing homework." He answered, making me laugh. He sounds just like Tori. Tori hated doing homework. I helped him with most of his college homework.

"Why is it hard?" I asked out of curiosity.

"No, I don't like bringing school home." His matter of fact tone made me laugh out loud and he looked up at me and giggled.

"You laugh funny." He said through his own laughing fit.

"I laugh funny? No you laugh funny." We both laughed until he started pointing out squirrels holding nuts. I never thought I would be so happy just walking with him, but I was.

After our walk around the park, we decided that it was time to drive over to Piedmont Hospital. They followed behind me in their car and we all parked in the hospital parking lot like I've done for the past few weeks.

"It'll be ok if you want to take him in the room while we wait in the waiting area." Todd offered. I thought that was nice and so I led them to the waiting area and Justin and I walked hand in hand over to Tori's room. I was so busy talking that I didn't see a woman with her back turned sitting by his bedside.

"Tori, you're going to be a dad, I'm pregnant." filled my ears as Lauren's voice became recognizable. My heart dropped to my feet and I paused in my tracks. I didn't want to scare Justin or even screw up this opportunity with my son so I coughed.

Lauren's head spun around quickly. The color drained from her face and she jumped out of the chair looking back and forth from both me and Justin. I was blocking her exit and a big part of me wanted to throw a punch at her face.

"I'm, I'm." She repeated before bolting out the door and down the hall. My ears felt like they were on fire. I couldn't believe her trifling ass was pregnant and by Tori. I needed to shake it off for now and get on with introducing Justin to Tori. I gently pulled Justin up to Tori's bedside.

"Tori, it's me Misha. I'm here with our son Justin. He came all this way to say hello." I started and Justin reached up and laid his hand on Tori's hand.

"Hi Tori." He spoke in a little voice like he was afraid to wake him.

"It's ok to talk to him Justin. He can hear you. He's been waiting a really long time to meet you and I'm sure he wishes he could tell you how happy he is that you came." I looked down at him as I spoke to him.

"Are you sure he can hear me?" Justin asked.

"Yes!" I answered enthusiastically, even though my blood was boiling. Justin pulled the chair up to the bed and climbed on it to help him get into the bed with Tori. I was totally shocked, but he laid down beside him and started telling him about his soccer games, how many goals he's scored, how he can't wait til Tori wakes up, so he can play soccer with both him and Todd. He explained how all of his friends said he was cool for having two dads. I sat in the chair and just listened to him go and on.

Just like before, tears began to drop from Tori's eyes and I knew he was listening to our boy talk to him. I decided to forget about Lauren for a moment because I wouldn't allow her or anyone else to rob me of this moment. I've waited too long for it to get here. We spent an hour and a half talking and laughing before I told Justin that it was time to go. He kissed Tori on his cheek and said for him to get better soon. That brought tears to my eyes. We walked hand in hand back to the waiting area where I told Megan and Todd that I was planning on staying a little while longer. I stooped to my knees and for the first time held onto my son like I wanted to and kissed his cheeks and hugged him. The damn finally broke loose and I cried as I held him. Justin waited a moment before asking.

"Why are you crying? We're going to see each other again right mom?" He looked up at Megan who smiled and nodded her head yes.

"I'm sorry, I'm crying because I'm so happy I got a chance to see you." I wiped my eyes and kissed him again. "I'm going to write you a letter and maybe if you'd like you can write me back, ok?" I asked and he agreed before they finally took him toward the elevator to leave the hospital. I was so sad and happy at the same time. What a day. I walked back to Tori's room determined to speak what was on my mind though.

"He's so beautiful Tori, you would have loved to see him and he's smart too. He's ours and he knows us now. I need you to come back to us, okay?" I started, but I wasn't finished. "I also want you to know I heard what Lauren's trifling ass said to you about being pregnant. If she thinks she's going to come in here and destroy my home again, I will kill her this time." I whispered into his ear. I needed him to hear me and clear. I wasn't about to allow it to happen again, not without a fight. I'd be damned if she got in the way of my family again, pregnant or not.

If Ever a Time
Tori

I heard Lauren's words, but more than that I could hear Misha talking in the background. I knew she was coming and I was panicking in my insides. When Lauren said she was pregnant, I wanted my heart to stop for a brief moment. I wanted to cause the machine to flat line to create a diversion. I didn't want Misha to hear, but I knew it was too late because seconds after it was said I heard the cough and then Lauren scramble out of the room. *If ever there was a time to be in a coma, it was now,* I thought to myself. I hoped that Misha wouldn't' cause a scene; but when she didn't, I felt almost like I could breathe. Then she introduced me to my son and my world came crashing down. I hated that I couldn't move until I felt him climb onto the bed. He talked to me like he already knew me. He shared his life with me and the love I had for him, though I couldn't see him, welled up until it overflowed in the form of tears. I knew Misha could see them because she wiped them with her fingertips.

I was grateful that she made little jokes, so I could hear him laugh. I loved that he loved sports. I was at peace listening to him talk to me. When he kissed me good-bye and told me to get better, I answered by saying I will just for you. I knew I had to fight this. I thought they were gone until I heard Misha come back and began talking again. When she mentioned hearing about Lauren, something in me snapped. I knew that if I didn't will myself out of this Misha would try to kill Lauren and I'd lose her all over again. She stayed a little longer before kissing me on the forehead and leaving again. Something was coming and it would be soon.

Caught Slipping
Lauren

I was so angry leaving the hospital that I could barely put the car in drive to leave. Chris was supposed to send me a message if he saw someone coming to the room, but he was nowhere to be found when I left. I couldn't believe that she walked in at the very moment I shared my pregnancy news with Tori. Now I would have to start looking over my shoulders because I already knew she was crazy. As soon as I got a few blocks away from the hospital, I called Chris.

"Hello?" He answered.

"What happened to you? His wife came to the room while I was still there!" I shouted in frustration.

"Look Lauren, I dig you, but I'm not wit that shit okay?" He spoke like we were friends and not boss and employee.

"Not with what?" I asked as if I didn't know.

"I'm not with you putting yourself out there for a married dude. His ass is in a coma anyway so what good is he? You need to realize you have a good dude waiting here for you, but I swear I won't wait forever." He lectured. I couldn't believe he wanted to choose now to go off on me. I didn't need this.

"I won't ask you to do anything else for me." I spoke into the phone.

"See there you go, I didn't say that, but I'm not doing nothing else that includes that dude." He responded. I ended the call on that note. I didn't like hearing him telling me no. I didn't feel like going home, so I stopped by my dad's to check on him. After my intervention, he rehired Mary and she's been actively keeping his house cleaned. She also sends me a text if she sees him have more than two drinks. I pay her a little extra for being my eyes and ears.

I used my key to get in and Mary was in the dining room wiping down the tables while my dad was watching television in the living room.

"There she is!" He belted out.

"Hey dad, hi Mary." I greeted them both.

"How are you honey?" He asked holding out his arm for me to sit with him on the couch. I flopped beside him.

"I'm fine." I lied resting my head on his shoulder.

"You hungry?" He asked. I nodded my head yes.

"Mary, can you make my daughter and grandchild a sandwich and something to drink?" My dad asked with a huge smile on his face. He loved the idea of a baby to spoil. I wasn't feeling so sure anymore, not with Misha finding out before Tori was awake to declare he was ready to leave her.

I ate lunch with my dad and watched a few soap operas before getting up to leave. I told him he needed to get back into the dating game and forget about Shannon. She was probably somewhere laid up with another man by now anyway. I wanted to get home to take a nap before I would need to get ready for my club tonight. I looked around before getting into the car, there was no one around. The drive back to my place felt like a long one and I was ready to just go home and lock the doors cause I damn sure didn't want her to catch me slipping again.

The Good News
Misha

I was a few minutes from my mom's house when my cell began to ring. I lifted it from the cup holder and saw Piedmont Hospital's number on the screen.

"Mrs. Carter?" a female voice asked.

"Yes." I answered.

"We need you to come back to the hospital. You're husband has come out of his coma and he's asking for you." The nurse gave me the good news. I almost swerved off the road before pulling over to collect myself. I couldn't believe what I was hearing. I did a U-Turn and headed back up to the hospital. I practically ran back to his floor and into his room. When I walked in, he was sitting up with his eyes open. Tears welled up in my mine and I almost choked trying to swallow the huge lump in my throat. I ran up to his bed and wrapped my arms around him.

"Don't you ever scare my ass like that again." I spoke into his ear. For the moment Lauren and all of her nonsense was at the back of my mind. I was just glad to see Tori awake. He coughed and put his hand to his mouth.

"My throat is dry." He spoke low. I looked around for his pitcher of water and poured him a cup before I brought it to his mouth. He drank like a man who was in a desert for months. A nurse came in and said it's normal for him to be thirsty, but not to let him over do it.

"I have to call your mom and sister." I said to him. I felt timid and amazed that I was actually talking to him while he was awake.

"In a minute." His voice came out raspy. He raised his arms slowly for a hug and I fell into his arms and let my tears wet his hospital gown. He started to cry too and it broke my heart before putting it back together.

"I want to see him." He stated. I knew he was talking about Justin, so I reached inside of my purse and took out his picture. He examined it for a moment before saying.

"He's a pretty handsome kid, huh?" I couldn't help but laugh because I knew he saw himself in Justin.

"Yeah, except he has his daddy's big ole' head." I joked.

A few doctors came back into the room and let me know they needed to run a few tests on him to be sure everything was ok. I felt fine with that, but I was scared to leave his side. Now that I had him back I didn't want to lose him again. While they prepared to take him to get an MRI, I gave his mom and sister a call and told them the good news. They both screamed in my ear and said they were on their way. I called my mom and told her that he woke up, but I let her know she didn't have to come up right away cause they would be running tests on him. I was excited to have him back. He asked the doctors if I could go with him for his test, which let me know he was scared too.

Today was one hell of a day. I got to meet my son, my husband came out of his coma, and I learned that my ex best friend was carrying my husband's baby. I just hoped God had a plan that didn't include me going to jail for murder.

By the time his mom and sister got to the hospital, he was already done his MRI. We were waiting for transport to escort him back up to his room. Both his mom and sister kissed and hugged him repeatedly. It wasn't until we got back to his room that he started to tell us that he heard us talking to him. He let us know that he felt locked within himself and wanted to desperately let us know he wasn't dead or dying. That made me cry, knowing that he felt that way. We told his mom about meeting Justin and showed them his picture. His sister kept saying, 'Oh my

God Tori." Cause he looked so much like him it was insane.

Aside from the fiasco with Lauren, I felt like today was a beautiful day. They didn't go home until visiting hours were over, but I stayed behind. There was no way I was leaving his side now. When we were left alone, I climbed into his bed and laid my head on his chest.

"So you heard everything, huh?" I asked.

"Yes." He answered. I knew he knew what I was referring to. I left it right there for now. We didn't have to discuss it right away. I just wanted him to know it was on the table, so we were going to come back to it later. He understood because he didn't say anything else about it.

"I'm going to quit my job so I can take care of you." I told him. He just wrapped his arms around me to let me know he was happy about that. "And I'm going to move back into the house." I continued.

"Ok." He answered.

Settling Matters
Tori

It's been eight weeks since I've been out of my coma and five weeks since they've let me come home. For the most part Misha has been moving some of her things bit by bit every day. I told her not to leave her job just yet, but to use her checks to add to our savings for now. She sold off all of her furniture at the apartment and we're just maintaining the rent until her lease is up in a few months. My job has given me a medical leave of absence until the doctor gives me the all clear to get back to work. I haven't talked to Lauren since she told me she was pregnant when I was in my coma. When Misha and I talked about it, she let me know she wouldn't stop me from seeing the child, but she won't be participating in it. I understood her position, but something in me wouldn't come to terms with the pregnancy until Lauren got a DNA test done.

I did a little research and decided I would call her at Club Seduction. The one place I knew she would be on a Friday night. Her office line rang and rang until finally a female voice answered.

"Thank you for calling Club Seduction this is Lauren." She answered.

"Lauren, its Tori." I paused. I could hear her breath catch in her throat. I was pretty sure she thought I was still in a coma.

"Tori, oh my goodness, when did you?" she started to ask, but I interrupted her this wasn't a social call.

"Listen, I've been doing some thinking and wanted to let you know that I will take care of my responsibility, but as far as you and me goes, it's not going to happen."

"But Tori, listen." She started up again, but I cut her off again.

"How many months are you?" I asked.

"Three and a half." She answered dropping her voice in frustration. I knew she wanted to get in my ear, but I didn't have time to hear all that.

"Good cause I did some research and we can do a Prenatal DNA paternity test." I finished it was her turn to cut me off.

"What the fuck are you trying to say?" She snapped.

"C'mon on with that. We both know you were fucking both me and Arnold's old ass, so I want to make sure that I'm taking care of my seed. I don't have a problem taking care of what belongs to me, but I'm not doing shit unless you take the damn test." I yelled into the phone receiver. I could hear her crying in the background, but I didn't give a damn. I couldn't afford to be putting my family through all this for no reason.

We were finally seeing Justin once a month and he was growing with the idea of having two sets of parents and I wasn't about to take her words on nothing.

"Fine, but it's for nothing though and I'm not paying for it, so you better figure that out." She snapped into the phone. I knew she didn't give much fight because she knew I wouldn't back down.

"I don't mind paying for it. I'll schedule the appointment and we can take it from there. Is there any time that you prefer?" I asked, sure I was getting under her skin.

"Anytime during the day is fine by me." She said with an attitude.

"Will we be there together?" She asked sounding hopeful.

"Yeah. Me, you, and Misha will be there together." I answered, but she slammed the phone down in my ear. I didn't have time to care. I was thinking with my brain instead of my little head this time around.

I would have to make the appointment tomorrow morning if they were open on Saturdays and then give

Lauren a call back to tell her the address, date, and time. I had a few other things I wanted to settle now that I felt strong enough to get around. I lost a lot of weight, but it was starting to come back now that I was able to eat real foods again. I planned on checking Eric for coming on to Misha while I was down. She didn't tell me he did anything, but if I knew him I knew he tried and I damn sure wasn't done with Arnold's ass either. He would get a taste of both my wrath and my vengeance. For a time that was all I could think of when I had nowhere else to go and nothing but time and my imagination.

Paternity Matters
Lauren

So many emotions ran through me when I heard Tori's voice. I couldn't believe he was out of his coma, but I also couldn't believe he was healthy enough to call and talk to me. He didn't let me get a word in and that pissed me the hell off, but overall I was happy he was at least alive. I didn't care about taking the paternity test because I was sure Tori was the father of my baby. I knew once he heard the news his heart would soften and he would look at Misha as a lost cause. How could he look at the mother of his child in the face and not fall in love with me? That was my hope and I planned on holding onto it until we were back together.

Now that my belly is growing enough to see a baby bump, I decided to tell Charles who went from being a perfect gentleman to a rude ass in a matter of minutes. He let me know clearly that he was sterile and couldn't have children, so I dropped his ass and didn't look back. It was fun while it lasted and my wardrobe, shoe collection, and club appreciated his contributions. I didn't quite have the heart to tell Chris outright about being pregnant until one of the female employees at the club asked me if I was pregnant in front of him. I wanted to deny it, but I just smiled and said, 'Yes, how'd you guess?' causing Chris to storm off angrily. I knew he'd get over it. He knew I was with other people so he really didn't have any reason to be upset.

I hung up on Tori when he said he was going to bring Misha to the DNA testing appointment because I really wanted to spend time alone with him again. We were once so good together and he just needed to be reminded of it. I stayed in my office most of the night monitoring the activity from the security cameras. I spotted Chris standing around sulking in front of a few customers. Some of the girls were trying to persuade him to dance, but he kept shaking his head no. I thought that was interesting because he would normally do one dance before walking off laughing at the over eager chicks trying to offer him up the goods. When the night finally ended, he brought all of the money into the office and dropped it on the table and turned to walk out.

"Chris wait." I stopped him. He paused, but turned to face me slowly.

"You're not going to help me count it?" I asked surprised.

"Naw, not tonight I have plans." He remarked sarcastically and continued walking out the door. He had plans many other nights, but it never stopped him from helping me out. I sulked behind my desk as I counted the money and placed it in stacks before putting it in the blue deposit bag. I marked the bag with the night's earnings and walked out to my car, tossing the bag in the trunk. I never kept it in the front with me. I didn't notice Chris watching for me to get in my car before he pulled off until after I saw his car's headlights go on. I smiled because though he was mad he still cared enough about my safety.

I drove home to my empty condo. My mom was given a project that she seemed to love doing. She was in charge of decorating the baby's nursery. I gave her a credit card with a fifteen thousand dollar limit and she was having a blast buying a crib, borders, changing tables, and baby clothes. We didn't have the sex of the baby yet and I had an appointment for an ultrasound coming up in a week so she used neutral colors. My shoes were removed before I stepped out of the Mercedes and I placed them beside the door. I hired one of Mary's cousins to help with housekeeping because I hated doing chores and she would also free up a lot of my time when I have the baby.

I undressed and slipped on a pair of boy shorts and a t-shirt and curled up in my bed. I held onto my full body pillow as if it were Tori like I have been doing for the last few weeks. Tonight felt better because I finally got to hear his voice and I knew that I had a chance, me and my baby had a chance. I allowed myself to sleep in and didn't get up until I heard my mom humming to herself as she left the kitchen to make her way into the baby's room.

"Good morning sleepy head." She kissed my forehead as she passed me in the doorway to my bedroom. "I laid out some fresh fruit on the counter and there is French toast in the microwave. Did you sleep ok?" she asked on her way up the stairs.

"Yes, I slept ok." I stretched and walked into the bathroom to brush my teeth and wash my face.

"You're here early." I said over my shoulder.

"Early? Its eleven o'clock already." She answered. I ran back into my room to check my phone. It was really that late. I tucked my phone in my bra not wanting to miss any possible call from Tori. Now that I knew he was awake again, I didn't care if he wanted to talk about paternity matters because the baby was his.

Lingering Guilt
Misha

The last few weeks have been pretty amazing. I've been trying to piece my life back together with Tori and he convinced me that now wasn't a good time to leave my job. As of now I've been running back and forth to get my clothes and things I want to keep and bringing it back to the house. I've learned quite a bit from Mr. Rosen, but even more from Arnold. Though Chris said he was going to handle it, Arnold still managed to come to work every day, smug and ready to talk his way out of a courthouse. It was good I guess for now. He has gone on to treat me like I am invisible, which I am extremely grateful for.

    I sat at my desk, searching through law books to help with Mr. Rosen's current legal case. He called me in to do some overtime this Saturday. He is defending a man they say killed his wife while she was sleeping. The odds were not in his favor, but he told me those were the best cases to win. I believed him because he always made sure to reward me with a new gift card, or a miniature bonus once the trial was over. After I jotted down a few notes complete with page numbers, I stood to walk them into his office. Knocking twice, I heard him tell me to come in. I saw that he was on the phone, so I waved the notes twice and sat them in front of him on the desk. Before I left, he covered the phone's receiver and asked.

"How is everything with your husband?"

"Fine, he's adjusting nicely and thank God he is still heathy." I answered giving him a quick update.

"Good, good well let me know if you need anything." He answered before going back to his call.

That was the last of my duties so I straightened up my desk before punching out of my phone and transferring his calls to the answering service. I planned on making a trip to the apartment to gather a few more of my boxes.

When I got there, Eric was outside waiting as he's done for the last two weeks.

"What are you doing here?" I asked not really surprised.

"I figured you still need my help." He answered, standing up from the steps. We both turned around at the sound of car coming into the parking lot. It was a cab with Tori seated in the back. My heart nearly jumped out of my chest and Eric's face read irritation. Tori stepped out and paid the taxi.

"Hey man!" He walked over to Eric and for a second I thought it was to hit him, but he offered his hand to shake. Eric grudgingly took it.

"What Misha called you over here to help?" Tori asked looking back and forth at us both. Eric didn't answer for a long moment.

"Naw, I knew she still had some things to move so I came through to see if she needed my help." Eric answered.

"Well, I appreciate that, but I'm here now, so you can roll out." Tori gave him a stare down that made me feel uncomfortable, but Eric didn't back down.

"Listen, I understand what you're saying, but it might not be a good idea for you to lift anything too heavy." Eric had a point, but if I knew Tori I knew he wouldn't take heed to anything Eric had to say.

"We're cool." I didn't want to interfere or it would look like I was taking Eric's side. I had to pick my battle and right now this wasn't one.

I pleaded with Eric through my eyes, begging him to let it go, but I knew he was thinking about Tori's pride causing me to pay by lifting all the boxes alone.

"I know you're cool, but all I'm saying is let me help you out a little. If you can do it, I'll fall back, but if you need me I'm here." He looked at me as he said that which infuriated Tori.

"Did you just look at my wife when you said that? Yo, homie it's time for you to take your ass away from here." He elevated his voice.

"Please Eric, just go ok?" I interrupted before things out way out of hand. Eric shook his head and walked back over to his car.

"You's a fool, Tori. You about to make your wife carry everything down because of ya pride." When Eric sat in his car and drove off, I felt relieved. I didn't want him to accidently mention what happened between us. I knew that possibility would be higher if a shouting match took place. I didn't want to tell Tori what I did, but I couldn't help feeling guilty. I shook the feeling and led me and him upstairs to my semi-empty apartment. Because his ribs were still healing, he wasn't really allowed to carry anything heavy, but he lifted a box of my clothes to prove he could. He carried the box to the car in silence even though pain was very clearly written across his face. I waited until the box was in the trunk before leaning into him and kissing him softly.

"What's that for?" He asked pulling me into him.

"For no reason. I love you is all." I smiled up at him and kissed him again.

"Hey Mish, I made an appointment for Lauren to take a Prenatal DNA Paternity test and I wanted you to be there when I go. It's on Tuesday, you think you can make it?" He asked me and I was surprised. I never heard of that being done during pregnancy.

"What time is it scheduled?" I asked

"Around noon, I tried to make it during your lunch break. It's not too far from where you work." He filled me in. Even though I didn't want to be anywhere near Lauren's hoe ass, I decided to go to support him and also let her know that he was still mine.

"Okay." We went back up to the apartment to load up two more boxes. I, of course, carried the heavier of the two and silently wished he would have let Eric help out.

Testing, Testing and Then Results
Tori

Tuesday couldn't get here fast enough. I felt nervous about finding out if Lauren's baby was mine. I knew that if Misha started to add things up I would be in serious trouble. I didn't mention us having that last session in the car when I was telling her to get her mom out of my mother in law's house. I was taking a huge gamble having them both in the same room. With Lauren stuck on trying to make us work, she might be desperate enough to say anything. I prayed which was more like begged God to keep things cool until I could figure it out. I took a cab over to Misha's job because I wasn't medically cleared to drive again yet and the insurance company from the other driver was still investigating before they sent me a check to pay me for another car.

When I got there, she was already waiting for me outside. I paid the cab driver and walked up to greet her. I held her an extra moment.

"Does the hoe know where to go?" She asked sarcastically.

"I called her and told her the information so she should be there." I answered. Misha got behind the wheel and I put the address into her gps. We arrived ten minutes later. I spotted Lauren's red Mercedes parked out front. The last time they were in the same room together was at the hospital and they were only cordial because Justin was there and Misha was being responsible.

When we walked into the clinic, Lauren was already there standing at the counter. She filled out her paperwork and when I arrived they took my payment first and then handed me a clipboard. The entire procedure came up to $1500. I filled out the necessary information and ten minutes later they called me back into a room to swab the inside of my mouth. Lauren was called to the back into a separate room where they did a blood test by a guided ultrasound to collect DNA from the fetus and the blood surrounding the placenta. The whole procedure was done in less than an hour.

Thankfully, no one said anything to each other and we were told we would have the results in five to seven days. I opted to have mine mailed to me. Spending the $1500 was nothing compared to what it would cost to raise the baby once it was here. I was just glad to have it done and out the way. When we left the clinic, Misha drove me home, I wasn't expecting it.

"Where you going?" I asked.

"Taking you home. I already talked to my boss about today, so he said I could come back when everything was finished." She explained. "Did you see her trying not to look in my direction?" She continued to ask.

"Yeah, but its cool honey. I'm glad you didn't say nothing to her cause I didn't feel like breaking up a fight." I commented, but I knew I was more grateful than anything else. She dropped me off and went back to work, leaving me with my thoughts.

I was a bit conflicted about the issue. If the baby was mine, I would be happy because I wanted children, even though I wanted them with my wife. But then if it wasn't mine, it would allow us to be free of Lauren for good. The next few days would be hell.

The days dragged with Misha become more and more irritable. I knew she was more nervous about the baby being mine than I was. She didn't let me make love to her and she barely wanted to kiss me. I didn't make a big deal because I tried to put myself in her shoes. I didn't expect to get the results until the seventh day, so when I got a large manila envelope with the clinic's name on it I froze. The first thing I talked myself into doing was calling Misha at work.

"Hello?" She answered like normal.

"Babe, the results are back." I stated.

"Did you open them?" She asked with curiosity.

"No, I was going to wait for you. Do you want me to do it when you come home?" I asked though I wasn't really sure if I could wait that long.

"No, give me one minute. I want you to read them to me over the phone." I could hear her get up from her desk and start walking. "Ok, I'm ready." She came back on the line.

I tore open the envelope slowly. My heart was beating through my chest. My fingers were trembling and right before I glanced over the page Misha said in a whispered voice.

"Wait, Tori listen. I'm scared because if that bitch is pregnant with your baby, I don't think I can take it."

"Don't make me nervous Misha. Shit!" I didn't want to think about the results breaking me and my wife up for good. I let my eyes focus on the words. They read: 0% possibility the child Lauren was carrying was mine. I screamed into the phone.

"The baby's not mine!" I was too excited. I could tell Misha was crying and I wished I was there to hug her.

"Ok, I gotta get back to work, but I love you and I'll see you when I get in." She said before hanging up.

I was done with Lauren for good this time and now I didn't have a lifelong commitment I would be forced to keep with her.

Speechless
Lauren

My mom stood in the room with me as the doctor rubbed a cold liquid jelly on my belly. We were having the first ultrasound done. I was so excited couldn't hardly breathe. When she pressed into my stomach using a scope connected to a long tube with the ultrasound machine on the other end, the baby came to life. My mom oohed and aahed at the small clump of cells in my stomach indicating a baby was there. The doctor kept moving it around to try to get a different picture. Then she stopped moving altogether.

"I believe I'm hearing two heartbeats." She said before putting it up to my stomach again. My heart nearly dropped.

"What!" I declared out loud. My mom put her hand to her mouth.

"Lauren look at that." My mom said excited. I didn't want to look at anything that said I was carrying twins.

Before the doctor had a chance to confirm, I could clearly hear both heartbeats. They were strong thumps that said they were fighters, survivors. Tears welled in my eyes. I couldn't believe that I was giving Tori two children instead of one. After the ultrasound, the doctor gave me a photo of the twin's sonogram. My mother wanted to look at it the entire ride home.

"I think we should start a scrapbook for them." I was trying to wrap my mind around one and they said I was having two. I don't think I am strong enough to go through with this. Then I thought about Tori and how happy he would be when he found out about the twins. It made me smile. When I pulled up to the gate, I punched in my code and waited for the gate to let me enter. My mom got out after I parked and got the mail.

I walked in behind her and noticed the large manila envelope with the clinic's information on it. I ripped it open excited to see what I already knew. However, the words 0% possibility of Tori Carter being the father jumped out at me. I felt more than weak at the knees. I flopped down on the couch, hot tears streaming down my face.

"What's the matter?" My mom asked still holding the black and white picture of the twins in her hands.

"Nothing, I wiped at my eyes. I'll be back." I took the sonogram and the results and walked to my room. There was only one other possibility and I hated the idea of it. Arnold was the father of my children and it was the worst mistake of my life. I sat on my bed contemplating what would be next move until I hit the speed dial button to Arnold's home office. It rang once, twice, a third time before a woman answered. I hesitated for a moment, the words not forming in my throat.

"Mrs. Blake?" I asked.

"Yes, who is this?" She asked.

"My name is Lauren Michaels and I'm calling to tell you that Your Husband is My Man!"

Made in the USA
Middletown, DE
05 January 2016